PLAY WITH ME

THE ATLAS COLLECTION (BOOK 5)

SAPPHARIA MAYER

EIDYLLIO

Ebook ISBN: 978-1-64893-012-6

Audiobook ISBN: 978-1-64893-014-0

Print ISBN: 978-1-64893-013-3

PLAY WITH ME

AUTHOR'S NOTE

Dear reader,

I am so glad you picked up my book, and I hope you enjoy the story it weaves. Please remember, theses books are works of fiction. The timelines are compressed, the interactions are dramatic and characters often jump into things for want of adventure.

You, dearest reader, live in a reality where the world is often stranger than fiction and a good dominant or submissive is hard to find. When you do find one, it is quickly evident they are imperfect humans who can't read minds, are less observant than one might prefer, and the interaction with them takes time. Like all things in life, communication is the key to any good interaction. The more authentically open you can be with a partner the more fulfilling the relationship.

Remember you are in charge of your life. Use your safe word, let others know where you are, know what aftercare looks like for you, use protection and have fun. The goal is to live in a beautiful safe, sane and consensual relationship with all parties pulling their weight. It is my hope you all find your special someone, just like the characters in my books. *~Sappharia*

WARNINGS & DISCLAIMERS

WARNING:

This book contains sexually explicit scenes and adult language. It may be considered offensive to some readers. This book is for sale to adults only, as defined by the laws of the country in which you made your purchase.

DISCLAIMER:

Please do not try any new sexual practice, without the guidance of an experienced practitioner. Neither the publisher nor the author will be responsible for any loss, harm, injury, or death resulting from use of the information contained in this book.

CHAPTER ONE

An eerie calm. Emotions recede. A deep breath comes. My voice is but a whisper. The cool crisp of logic infuses itself into every pore. Details I would let go mere minutes ago are now important. Each one better be perfect. For greater men than you have beat the emotions out of me until all I knew was perfection through annihilation.

Emotion is illogical. It takes much to get me to the place where I am open, and they flow freely. I must work to be open, no matter how much I desire to do so. It is a labor.

The fastest way usually comes when I have failed, for they use emotions to beat me into submission. The crashing waves of all the things I've missed, all of my failure and realization of my worst fears. Under it, my knees buckle, and I release.

I want there to be another way, but too many situations, too many people use it against me. Release is sometimes such a wonderful thing. Other times it stokes a different fire. It is all in the path to get there and the safety I find.

But now... now is not the path of positive positions. Now is the path past anger. Filled with protection. Focused from the words beginning to whisper through my thoughts.

"Emotions make you weak."

"Keep this up and you will prove to be the failure I already know you are."

"No one wants to be with an emotional woman!"

"So men are better, they are stoic and strong." "

Women are less because they use emotions to manipulate situations."

"Men are always more successful because they are logical and can think in a crisis."

I've heard them all and then some. There were times I hit my knees and did not think I would get up as the emotions swirled through me. Then I learned the cold, cruel calculation of logical thought. It does not care about you, nor does it attach any emotion to your situation. Through its lens, you are an object who threatens to harm my world. Every fuzzy detail becomes clear. Question more pointed. My entire world is a deep breath of calm. My patience is thin, and observation is even higher than normal. Here, I will take mass casualties to ensure damage because yours will match mine. It is a game of chicken, chess and go. Each one with a different aim and strategy. >

My voice is now but a whisper, as a smile slides across my face. Harm to one I love now ends my level of patience, anger and sleepless nights it cost me to get here again. Every lesson I've learned now trains every skill on one goal. Your move. Greed got you here. Emotions can't save you. And I've got lots of time- do you?

I'll send your regards to the men who taught me those lessons before you.

Emotions are weakness, and I am not.

The knock at the door draws my attention, but I do not look up.

"Enter," I command, my pen finishing the last strokes with a flourish.

Katie enters the room and sets a cup of coffee on my desk, then picks up the cold one.

"My apologies for the interruption, Ma'am. Mr. Kinkaid is here to see you."

"Tell him I will find him later."

"She'll tell me no such thing," Kade says, his voice booming in an echo around the room. "You've scurried between three locations at all hours for the last month. We've all given you time and space, but enough is enough, Ma'am."

I lift my eyes. He stands in a perfect parade rest, his eyes forward in respect. Tension ripples through his muscles.

"I've got businesses to run, Thomas. He put my life, and the lives of others, in danger and on hold with his games. It left everything in shambles. Now I must catch up before it all falls apart," I reply with an icy tone as I place the fountain pen on top of the journal entry I was writing.

"With all due respect, you are surrounded with a capable team."

"You are all capable, but it is my responsibility. It stops on my desk. Every detail, every decision comes from me. No matter if I make them or not. Both as a Dominant and as a business owner," I say and push my chair back from the desk. The space is suddenly confining.

"If you'd continued to build your team, this situation would be easier," Dominick replies as he walks through the door. "I always thought Thomas would make a fine Major Domo and from the looks of this place, he was doing an excellent job at running your House while you were... indisposed."

"Dominick," I acknowledge.

I watch his eyebrow raise in a question, but he does not verbalize it.

"This isn't your concern," I continue. "Mr. Kinkaid ran the club, and some of its major events, with efficiency, but it is my understanding he struggled under the stress and the weight of them. It is unfair, as the head of this House-or club as it is in actuality, to unduly place such weight on the staff."

Kade does not move as Dominick walks behind him.

"I don't disagree that you failed. If you'd continued the correct course of training, provided the necessary skills to Mr. Kinkaid and the other staff members, the burden would not be as heavy. However, you chose this direction by your own actions. Now you must train others to take control while you learn to release it in the most dire times. A troublesome situation without doubt," Dominick says as he lowers himself into the chair to my right in front of the desk.

I pull my shoulders back and straighten. This is a battle of wills, and Dominick has a clear advantage of position and history.

"It's not your call," I state. "Mr. Kinkaid is capable. You are correct that I should expand his training in this job when the timing is better. For the moment, I am more than able to right this ship, so to speak."

"Pardon my disagreement," Ian says from the doorway.

I take a deep breath and sigh.

"As a fiscal investor in this enterprise," he says as his arms motion to the room and club, "I am in agreement with these two gentlemen."

"You are a thirty percent investor," I remind him.

"Fifty-two. Your absence caused a need for an influx of funds in several divisions of your enterprise, and I stepped in to help," Ian replies as he takes the seat beside Dominick.

Kade cringes.

"I'll discuss this with you later, Kade," I say through clenched teeth.

I take a deep breath to calm the swirl of emotions and reach for the next logical step.

"Gentlemen," I address them, "I appreciate your concern. Mr. Breckenridge, I will be glad to discuss our current business arrangements enacted in my absence. Mr. Dawes, your personal insertion into this matter has caused quite enough issues. Mr. Kinkaid, you and

I will discuss your decisions at length. Now, if you all will excuse me, there is a mountain of work which requires my attention."

"Your Southern hospitality is slipping. Along with its accent," Samantha quips as she walks into the office. "Just accept the help."

"Why does this feel like an ambush?"

"More like an intervention," Dr. Jillian Hart replies as she enters.

"Out! All of you. This is my office and my realm," I command.

"Hear us out, Alexandra. Give us an hour. We're here to help," Jillian replies and steps toward my desk.

I close my eyes and try to find my center. Work is my solace, even if it overwhelms me right now. All I need is for them to get out and let me do my job.

Pain radiates up my neck as the headache, which was building moments before, takes hold. I refuse to rub my temples, not giving them another inch into my world. I open my eyes, glance down at my desk, and center myself. With the last draw of strength, I smile and stand, pulling myself up to a perfect posture.

"Thank you all for your concern. This situation is tough for every one of us, in different ways. I never intended to affect you and an apology is far too little, too late. All I can do is ask for your forgiveness and patience," I say as I focus on maintaining the deep Southern accent indicative of Alexandra.

"Sit down," Dominick says in a menacing whisper. He hands Kade an envelope.

Kade steps forward, places it on my desk, and steps back to his original position.

"Take those before that headache of yours gets worse." Dominick nods to the envelope on my desk. "We expect you in the studio apartment above the PR firm in an hour. Failure to make the appointment in the appropriate 'identity' will be met with dire consequences. Do not push me on this, Alexandra."

Everyone nods in agreement. I focus an icy glare at Dominick. Nothing escapes his observation, and my frustration grows at the inability to hide the smallest issues.

"Not advisable," he states. "We'll see you in an hour."

Without another word, he stands and walks out the door. The rest of the group follows until only Samantha is left.

"How are you?" she asks, her tone soft and full of concern.

"I'm fine. There's a mountain of work, but I'll get it done or undone, whichever is more appropriate."

"Why?"

The simple question punches straight into my gut. It is laced with accusations and betrayal.

"My job is to protect you. All of you. No matter the cost," I reply in resignation.

"That's stupid."

I shake my head. "It's not. My personal honor code and duty call me to it."

"Your code is flawed. It's missing an important piece. One I am unsure how you've not learned," she whispers.

"And what is my code missing?"

"Family. Community. The acknowledgment of the people around you. All of who care for you. They are smart, intelligent, talented, and capable. It isn't you against the world, Alexandra. It is all of us pulling together and making it work. We all have difficulties. Every person here is full of strengths and weaknesses," Samantha continues. "How does an amazing Dominant and wicked smart business owner miss such a thing?"

"I see you've been hanging around Dominick too much," I try to joke.

"Yes. He's worried about you. We all are, but he's especially so."

"He gave up the right to worry about me when I moved to DC."

"Actually, you gave it back to him when you went to his brownstone for help. There's more to that man than meets the eye," Samantha says as she furrows her brow.

"I owe him a debt, but I am not his responsibility."

"First, I don't think he sees it that way. There's something about the entire thing which feels... off."

Curiosity blooms. Samantha's knowledge of Dominick runs as deep as mine, but he's always been a mystery to me, no matter how close we were.

"Off... how?"

"I don't know. There's something he's not saying and the whole thing with Cassandra is just... odd," she says as she stands and shakes her head. "Maybe I'm trying to make something out of nothing." Samantha shrugs.

"An intervention? Really?" I ask as Samantha walks toward the door.

"Yes. Really," she says over her shoulder as she leaves the office.

The headache blooms. I idly pick up the envelope as I stare out the window.

"I'm so tired of ambushes," I mutter.

CHAPTER TWO

I stare at the image in the mirror. Each layer I remove from Alexandra makes me more vulnerable as Atlas. It wasn't Alexandra who was on the boat or watched Reece bleed. And it definitely wasn't her who knelt when he commanded it. It's illogical to think of them as two different people, when in reality they are all me, but it stripped nothing from me as Alexandra. While it lays Atlas bare.

With a sigh of resignation, I reach up and pull my blond hair into a low ponytail. As I stand, I tug the knee-length cardigan around me. It's not much armor, but it will do for now. I glance at my watch. Five minutes until my execution. I walk to the tunnel door and click off the lights to Alexandra's dressing room.

I measure each stride as I try to calm the butterflies taking flight in my stomach. I realize they think they are right, but I am lost without Reece. Our time together shifted something in me, and I don't know if I like it.

I press the hidden bookcase door open and walk into the PR firm. A cacophony of voices assaults me as I step to the studio apartment staircase.

"What aren't you telling us, Dominick? And who is this?" Kade says so loud even I cringe.

The silence that follows, along with the recalcitrant "Yes, Sir" makes me almost laugh. I know the exact look Dominick is shooting across the room.

Seconds later the chatter is back up to a roar until I step into the apartment, and it shatters to silence.

"Good evening," I say with all the confidence I can muster.

"Welcome, Atlas. I'm glad you joined us," Dominick says from the leather chair on the far side of the seating area. Memories of dinner with Reece flood my mind, and I blink back the tears which threaten to spill.

I nod and take the empty leather seat opposite him. Around the room, everyone else is sitting on bar stools, the floor or the couch, with one exception. An unfamiliar person is propped on the windowsill. He turns to watch me as I sit. When his face comes into full view, an odd recognition dawns on me, but I refuse to acknowledge it.

"I see you've brought someone new into our midst for such a personal conversation," I accuse Dominick.

"It was necessary."

"Then you won't mind explaining it to the rest of the class," I reply with an audacity I do not possess.

"In due time. We were discussing your current situation," he says with a regal nod.

"Actually, I believe Kade was accusing you of not sharing information. Much the same way I just did."

"Indeed," he states.

I stare at him. Neither one of us flinches under the harsh gaze of the other.

"You'll lose this game, Atlas. I do not mind if it is in front of this group... do you?" he asks, raising an eyebrow.

I force my breath to remain steady, but I already know I will capitulate. For several minutes, I hold his gaze. The strain in the room increases, and no one dares to say a word. We lock in a battle of wills until his jaw tightens, then my eyes drop to the floor right in front of his feet.

"Good decision," Dominick praises me in a firm whisper.

When I lift my eyes, two pairs stare back with the same level of tension. It is the man behind Dominick I want to learn more about, because what I know doesn't make sense.

"Before it derails this meeting and its intended purpose, the gentleman behind me is Garrett. He is with a group called Obsidian Overwatch. They will be taking over the necessary personal protection duties," Dominick says and holds up a finger towards Kade, whose inhale reverberates around the room, but he does not take his gaze off mine. "This will allow everyone else more time to concentrate on all the other variables in play. Are there any logistical questions?"

I pause to give the rest of the group a chance to ask their queries. When none comes forth, I look past Dominick and to Garrett.

"Welcome to the Empyrean Club, Garrett. Please give Tess and Evan my regards," I say with a cynical smile. Garrett looks at the back of Dominick's head and then back to me. "He's not the only one with observational skills. Nothing goes on in my club without my knowledge."

Garrett chuckles and nods towards me but doesn't utter a word.

"What's with all the cloak and dagger, Dominick? I'm tired. I've got businesses to run and a call to make to Miami," I say as I let my body collapse into the soft leather chair.

"There's more at play here than our immediate concerns, but those explanations can wait. Dr. Hart, I would like you to sit down and evaluate Atlas' emotional and mental state. If you believe the services your friend Jacob White might prove helpful, don't hesitate to call him. Samantha, you will take on the duties of managing partner for McKenzie Kingston. Jessica, please get with Garrett and give him your findings. Kade, you will help manage the club," Dominick says, issuing his edicts without taking his eyes off of me.

"You can't do this," I say, staring at him in stunned anger.

"I can. All except for Drs. Hart and White. Those I will leave to them as I believe their expertise is beneficial for your own personal well-being. The rest, as per my agreement with the majority owner in all enterprises, is absolutely under my command."

Tears threaten to spill, but I hold on to my anger instead. I look around the room. Each person moves uncomfortably under my glare until I return it to Dominick.

"Bastard," I curse.

"Indeed," he agrees. "In addition, you will stay on premise in this residence until Garrett's team says otherwise. A body double will be stationed at your apartment to provide the illusion that you've returned to life as normal."

"You can't do this. If you knew anything about me..."

"I know everything about you, Atlas. You are stuck between more than two worlds with a stalker who wants you dead because you won't become his perfect obsession. No one thought it would end up the way it did down in the islands. We were all wrong, and I take full responsibility for it."

"Why?"

Dominick's lips pull into a thin line, and he steeples his fingers in front of them. He furrows his brows and then relaxes.

"Because we all make mistakes, and some are more costly than others," he replies. "Please don't fight me on this, Atlas. We both know I will win in the end, and the expense of resources is best used elsewhere."

"Because you're a man? We're both Dominants. Equal in every way. Even if we didn't carry the same status, you are not my better. So why do you think you'd triumph?"

A smile crosses his face, and he looks around the apartment.

"They will all ensure it because they care about you and know this is the best path forward for you."

"Traitors," I swear under my breath as I push out of my chair and then storm toward the kitchen on the other side of the suite.

With a yank on the refrigerator door, I peer inside and begin pulling out several platters of prepared food. "Dominick even controls dinner," I growl to myself.

"You remind me of Tess," Garrett says from behind me.

I startle and work to control my reactions.

"Would she be pleased if someone issued such edicts?" I ask as I unwrap the food trays and place them on the island.

Garrett chuckles. "Quite the opposite. She'd be furious and with much less grace."

"Do they know you're here?"

"No," he replies without elaborating.

For the next few minutes, he helps me prepare the trays for the group. The work helps keep my emotions in check. There's something soothing about being able to provide for those I care about. By the time we lay out the food, drinks and serving wares, sadness and annoyance fill me, but the motion dissipates the anger.

On the other side of the room, the tone of the conversations shift. Occasionally lilts of laughter float my way. From my vantage point, I look up and enjoy watching everyone gathered in one place. I never take time for such indulgence. No matter what else happens, I am glad for this moment.

"What's he not telling me, Garrett?" I ask when we've completed our task.

"It's not mine to share, Ma'am."

"He's placed you and your team as my personal security. Is there something I should be worried about?"

Garrett sighs and runs a hand through his hair.

"It's bigger than you. Which is unfair. In some ways, we're responsible for the expanse of the situation. They called me in to clean it up as quietly as possible."

"Wait. Edmund's been a client for the past few years. He wanted to expand his fantasy, and he asked me to marry him. I never thought he'd stalk me, but then again, I didn't tell anyone about it either. The only reason he increased his focus on me was because I didn't give in." I tell him the same story I've told myself a thousand times.

He nods. "Yes. That is where we are now," he agrees.

"Why do I feel an unspoken 'but'?"

"With all due respect, I've said more than I should have shared. My job over-watch in this situation, and I'm not at liberty to divulge any more information. No matter how unfair I think it is that you carry the burden of responsibility for the situation," Garrett said as he grabs a sandwich and walks back to lean against the window frame.

"I'm sorry Dominick was an ass," Samantha says from beside me.

I turn towards her, Garrett's words still running through my mind.

"It was less intervention and more royal decree. Looks like someone took my kingdom while I was gone and no one sent me so much as a carrier pigeon," I say, trying to keep the bitterness out of my voice.

"I didn't know he would rearrange your world. I'm so sorry. You know I don't want to be the managing partner of the chaos that is McKenzie Kingston."

"It's not chaos. You'll be fine," I say and force a smile to form.

One after another, each person comes by and gives their apologies. All except Dominick, who sits imperiously in the leather chair and watches.

CHAPTER THREE

The last of the team trickle out of the studio apartment with a final goodbye and I know it will be okay as they walk down the stairs to the firm's front door. All except Dominick and Garrett, who are both sitting in the same places.

I clean up the kitchen and let the patterns form across my mind. There's something I am missing, and I don't enjoy feeling behind the situation.

Mindlessly, I combine the food on to one platter. I spray the counters and clean the kitchen to relieve tension.

All I want is for things to go back to normal or almost normal. To find a balance between the comfort of my submission under Reece's guiding hand and the power I control in the worlds I've created around me.

Why did Garrett's organization sound familiar? The question interrupts the happy scene forming in my mind. It is an unwelcome intrusion that sends a shiver racing down my spine.

Obsidian... dark... truth enhancing... protective stone... draws out stress and tension... formed in the fire of a volcano. The word play continues as I reach deeper into my memories. Overwatch... to watch over... force protection tactic... observe terrain ahead... effective cover fire. Protective stone which watches over.

Every muscle tenses and I stop mid-movement. My breath comes in shallow waves as realization dawns. No! I want to scream, but if they are here, it's already too late. This isn't happening, I tell myself.

With a deep breath, I place the platter in the refrigerator and grab a bottle of wine. It will be smarter to keep my wits about me, but I'm done. Too many things stolen combine with too many restless nights. I grab a wineglass and pour a generous amount.

This isn't happening! I scream louder in my mind to drown out all the patterns now forcing their way together.

Dominick's sudden appearance. His push to understand why I was on his doorstep. The reminder of my training and roots in his house. If Garrett is with Overwatch, it's all far worse than I imagined. They recruit from the best covert organizations around the world, if that is even his actual name.

Act calm and normal, I command myself, intently aware of Dominick's and Garrett's presence. Neither one will miss the slightest change.

Do I let them know I know? Do I act ignorant of my knowledge? What's my next play? My mind races between panic and logical calm. I want to leave. It is the smartest play, but all of us know the only way to my release is when they allow it.

Edmund... I try to fit his name into the puzzle in front of me. I feel my brow furrow, and I know I've given away too much information, but it's important. How does Edmund fit into this situation? Why are they here now?

The patterns which formed moments ago disintegrate in my mind. Frustration reigns as the tension headache creeps along the back of my neck, pulsating at the base of my skull.

I take another large sip of wine and demand my body listen to me.

"Come sit, Atlas," Dominick commands from across the room.

I look up. His hand motions to the leather chair across from him. Garrett moves from the windowsill to the couch.

Like a death-row inmate, I walk to the chair, gripping my wineglass like a security blanket.

In a last effort to force my calm, I take a deep breath and lower myself into the chair.

I look Dominick in the eye and ask the only question which makes sense.

"Why is the Sovereign Society here, and what do you want?"

"See, Garrett, I told you she was the best of my trainees," Dominick says, pride lacing his voice. His fingers steeple in front of his mouth, but he relaxes his body.

"And I walked away from it," I say without taking my eyes off of him.

"A shame, too. I blame it on your father's expectation in the vanilla world and the fact you didn't want to jeopardize that relationship. Along with youth and your emotional aversion to the concept at the time. Though I'm sure if things were slightly different you might change your mind."

I take a long pull on my wine and wrap my thoughts around his confession while berating myself on not seeing it earlier. But what am I missing?

"Nothing," Dominick replies, and I pull my lips into a thin line in aggravation at the fact he answered a question I did not voice. "You're missing nothing, except the details to which you wouldn't be privy."

"You mean like what Edmund's proposal and stalking of me has to do with why one of the regional leaders of the Society is sitting in my studio apartment dismantling my life on a whim? Or why such a minor matter draws your attention at all?"

Dominick nods. "Let me take those in reverse order. What was the last thing I said to you when you left my household?"

Emotions flood through me as the memories race across my mind.

"If I was ever in trouble, you'd be there," I reply with an easy answer.

"Don't push me, girl," Dominick warns.

I glare at him and then relent.

"I bear the training mark of the Sovereign Society without regard of its completion to membership. In it, I am bound by the honor code to protect those around me and the duty to uphold the standards of my house. As such, I am forever in its debt and under its protection." I recite the words drilled into me so long ago.

"As you know from your studies, the Society continuously checks on its members, former members, and trainees. We operate on the edge of most governmental laws and societal customs. Somewhere between the shadows and plain sight."

I nod. "I never objected to the consensual contracting of humans to others or even of the selling of their contracts. The only reason I left was to prove to my father I was as capable as any boy. Even the baby I replaced," I reply without emotion.

"Really?" Dominick asks in surprise.

"Really," I confirm. "Good to know I still have my secrets."

Dominick chuckles.

"Now. Stop with this bullshit and tell me why you're here. If you aren't here for me or some area I overstepped, then why?"

"My house comes to you indebted. We did not honor our vow of protection, for it covers even when it is not requested..." Dominick replies.

Silence lingers.

"Say it, Dominick. You know it's not fair, and you are solely to blame for her burden. I, for one, am tired of it. My allegiance is to your house, but don't press me," Garrett demands.

"You two are making no sense." I look between them.

"Edmund's actions are ultimately our fault. We created the monster. You were his target to hurt us."

I stand up and pace through half the room.

"Care to explain how Edmund Hurter is your fault? He was my client. I missed the signs of his obsession with me. Which created... a more significant problem I thought I could control. It was my job to protect them." I shake my head at the memories of the past few months.

"Mr. Hurter was part of the Society," Dominick states.

I stop pacing and look at him. "Was?"

"As you know, few members are ever dismissed from our ranks. The intake process is extensive. On a rare occasion, we miss something. With Edmund, we missed everything."

"Define everything? He was always charming and a perfectionist in service. Until his marriage proposal, he was a gentleman," I reply, trying to find what I missed.

Dominick nods. "He fooled us all. The reason for his dismissal was his treatment of the contract owners. While he presented in a service and submissive position, they could never give him enough stimulation. He pushed for more than they desired and broke the codes by which we live. Over time his callousness and lack of remorse for his behaviors began to manifest as well as his charming gift for being a pathological liar. The problem is, he's brilliant. His current money was made because of his contract payout and abilities to present as something he's not. He controls his company through grandiose speeches and blames others for his actions when a short-term scheme fails. Corporate America is his best habitat."

"Let me back up. What do you mean he broke the code?"

Garrett clears his throat. Dominick glances down at the floor and runs his hand down his face.

"He tied his contract owners. They were a dominant male and female couple. They found the male in a strappado torture tie. His hands were tied behind his back and suspended by ropes around his wrist. He'd hung weight around his neck to make the position more painful. Ultimately, both shoulders were dislocated. On the other hand, he whipped the woman until she was bleeding, repeating the process several times. According to reports, he did several other unsavory things while lecturing her on the proper way to dominate a man."

A shiver races through my body.

"Obsidian was alerted to a possible problem after three days. A trial was held, but the decision was split. The couple refused to press formal charges, we presume based on threats he made, but their official record said he was acting on their orders," Dominick comments.

"Acting on their orders?" I ask, spinning on my heel.

"Yes. According to their statement, they were both pain-based masochists, and they were playing a game when Overwatch interrupted. The team leader reported they were relieved and seemed to fear for their lives."

"This sounds like a plot for a movie, not the actions of a client," I say as I shake my head. "If these things happened under the Society's watch, why is he here?"

"That's what I was investigating when Samantha called and said you were missing," Garrett replies. "He was in the California region at the time of the incident. A region's Regent is responsible for everything that goes on in their area. Edmund's name was different, and he slipped his check-ins. Somehow, we lost track of him. No one put his current identity with his former name until you showed up on my doorstep," Dominick says with a sigh.

I let his words penetrate my thoughts. The version of Edmund he described doesn't match the person I knew until the marriage proposal. It was the one thing which always puzzled me. Why a marriage proposal? I always thought it was an overblown infatuation.

"Why me?" I ask the one question I may not want answered.

"I am the last Head of House who voted against him. At current, you are the only person who trained in my house not to be a member of the Society. It is the working theory at least."

I nod my head in agreement, trying to find the logical thread.

"Then why a marriage proposal?"

"The only two ways to separate you from my house is a marriage outside of the Society or death," Dominick replies without letting his gaze leave mine.

My stomach clenches, and the world tilts as I grab the back of the chair to help me stand. Strong arms wrap around my waist.

"Easy now. We've got you," Garrett says as he gently helps me into the seat.

"That answers that question," Dominick says as he walks to the kitchen. The heels of his shoes click across the floor as he returns and hands me a glass of water.

"Your actions and lack of confidence nearly cost several lives," he starts.

"Now's not the time," Garrett growls at him. His hand never leaves my shoulder.

It is warm and firm. The last vestiges of my world shatter into shards of illusion. Things I thought I could handle were bigger than I saw. I am caught between two worlds, and I do not know which one to choose. If I even have a choice at all.

"I think that's enough for tonight," Garrett says.

"She needs to know everything," Dominick challenges.

Their voices barely penetrate my thoughts. I am numb. It's not the fall that hurts, as they say-it's the sudden stop at the end. It is as if my mind jumped off a skyscraper and just hit the sidewalk. Nothing makes sense. I don't know how to form a plan or my next move. At this moment I am both safe and vulnerable but in a way which forces an incongruent.

"And she will. You just gave her more information than anyone could absorb. It took us months to get a handle on this. You can't expect her to do it in an evening," Garrett shoots back.

"I can and I do."

"Unreasonable prick," Garrett mutters.

"Careful. I'll excuse your unprofessional behavior this time, but don't forget who I am and who she is to me."

Garrett sighs and his hand squeezes my shoulder lightly.

"Yes, Sir."

"Baiting him is the only move we've got right now."

"She can't do it. There's too much at stake."

I stare unseeing into the room. Thoughts refuse to form, and I drift further from the unpleasant reality. Unmoored. Lost at sea. Sail-boat. Reece.

A tear falls down my cheek, and I blink my eyes slow enough to stop the next one. I need you, Reece, I scream in silence. I can't do this alone, but you aren't safe with me.

The words tip my emotions over the edge, and a river of tears rolls down my cheek. I can't do this. Everything in me is tapped out. I don't move as my world implodes. I need you, Reece.

A click echoes in the room, but it doesn't draw my attention. The pressure on my shoulder from Garrett's hand is gone. The world is a bubble of indistinct noises overlapped by a conversation I no longer register.

"You're safe, Atlas. I'm right here." I imagine Reece's voice cutting through dissonance of the room noise and thoughts in my mind and try to focus, but struggle to re-engage the outside world.

"Breathe through it," I hear as I imagine what he'd tell me to do right now.

"Eyes on me." The words are a command and pull on my focus.

"Atlas... eyes on me!" Reece's voice penetrates the fog. I lift my eyes and stare into his, barely believing he's standing in front of me.

"Hello, beautiful."

CHAPTER FOUR

I struggle to understand what my eyes see.

"Breathe. Deep breaths. In and out. You're safe. I'm right here," Reece says without breaking eye contact. "Gentlemen, you are both dismissed. We can take this up tomorrow."

"I must object, Mr. Gabriel," Dominick starts.

"I don't care what you think you must do. I want you out, now," Reece growls through clenched teeth, but his gaze is soft.

The sound of footsteps fills the space, but he puts a finger under my chin to prevent me from turning my head to look.

"Looks like someone is at the end of her rope, face down in the mud, and still trying to lift the world," he quips.

"There's another way?" I croak.

Reece lifts an eyebrow and the last vestige of strength leaves my body.

"Sir."

He smiles down at me as the soft click of metal tells me we are alone.

"Kneel and let me lift your world, Atlas. Remember, that which yields is not always weak," he whispers.

His unexpected appearance is like being plucked out of the stormy sea as his words wash over me. I slide out of the chair and fold my knees under my body.

"Head to the floor," he commands when I attempt to look up at his leg.

My body follows his words without a fight, and I lean forward until the cool tile presses against my forehead.

"Good, girl."

His leg brushes against my body. The chair scrapes across the floor. Above me he moans as he settles. I cringe. His pain is my fault. This mess is my fault. No one can live in-between two worlds. Either you're in one or you're in the other. You can't have both.

"Overthinking as usual, I see," he states. There's no expectation of an answer. "It is my understanding that you've worked yourself hard since your return, even though you've led me to believe the opposite on our video chats." He sighs.

"While I don't always care for Dominick's tactics, he's right about you. It looks like I need to sit down with him and learn a thing or two."

I cringe at the thought, and at the same time I smile. It is a dichotomy of the duality of my nature. The need for both a hard hand and a soft kiss. A place where I own power and one where I give it to another.

"Tonight, I want to be with you. Hold you close to my chest and know you are safe... real. I've missed you, Atlas. You are definitely my undoing," he says. "Kneel up."

I pull my body up and push my shoulders back until I settle in the meditative position.

"Look at me," he prods.

Tears fall down my face as I look up at him. My failure is written on his body. I glance at the cane leaning against the chair, and my lip quivers.

"Stop it," he commands. "A madman did this, not you. There are many things you've done over the course of the last month to earn my ire, but this," he says, motioning to his leg and cane with his hand, "is not one of them."

I nod, not trusting my voice.

"Words, Atlas. They are important."

I take a shaky breath. "Yes, Sir."

"It's a start. There's a long road ahead of us, but you're one of the strongest women I know, and this time, we'll all help you lift the burden."

"Thank you." I force the words out in a whisper.

"Now get off the floor. I want you in bed and naked in five minutes. It's been too long since I've held you," he says and smiles down at me.

"Indeed. I've missed you, Reece."

I rise from the floor in an awkward push. Every limb is gangly and uncoordinated as I try to avoid bumping into his leg. The memories of the night flood through me. He could have died. Icy fingers of dread caresses my spine. The image of his body lying lifeless on the bow of the boat makes me bite my lip to hold back the emotions. For the last month I buried myself in my work, sure he'd walk away.

"Please don't leave me." The words slip out.

Reece grabs my arm and stops my forward movement. He pulls himself out of the chair and stares down at me.

"I'm not going anywhere, Atlas," he says.

His hand tightens around my arm as if he's afraid I'll vanish.

"You're the most important thing in the world to me. This problem brought a clarity I didn't know I lacked. I don't care what you are or what you do. I need you in my life, and more importantly, I want you there."

I shake my head. "Things are complicated, Reece. I'd give up everything for you. You need to know that is a fact. But I'm not sure how this will end, and I won't put you in danger again."

"My life isn't your choice. It's mine. We'll sort it all out tomorrow. Right now, all I want is to feel your mouth on my cock. To hold you close and wake up with you in my arms tomorrow. Do you think you can handle that command?" he asks as he lowers his forehead to mine.

"Yes. I think that's the easiest command I've ever heard."

"Good, then let's deal with the rest tomorrow. Now, strip," he commands and chuckles when my hands eagerly wrap around the top button of my shirt.

With each step I loosen a button until my shirt is open and I push it off my shoulders, letting it fall to the floor. Next I unhook my bra and continue the slow processional to the bedroom, as I leave a trail of clothes behind me.

The soft click of Reece's cane tells me he's not far behind. When my panties fall to the floor, I hear him gasp behind me.

"Mine," he growls as he steps behind me. "Stand by the bed."

Reece steps around me and sits on the edge as he tosses his cane to the floor.

"Come here."

I step towards him, putting his face level with my breasts.

"These are mine," he says as he lowers his head.

His tongue licks across my left nipple before biting down. The cut of pain and heat flare across my body. My pussy clenches in need. Reece swirls his tongue again before sucking on the tight bud. Casually, he moves to the other breast and gives it the same treatment. He continues at a languid pace like a man enjoying a feast after being starved for far too long.

"Did you miss me?" he asks right before his teeth clamp around my nipple.

The mix of sensations along with his dominance release the last weight from my world.

"Yes, Sir." The words tumble from me. Everything about them is right.

"On your knees," Reece says in a soft command.

I nod and sink to my knees, grasping the bed for support. Reece grasps a handful of hair, and I sigh.

"Home."

I nod in agreement.

"Touch me. Don't be afraid. I want to feel your hands and mouth on me until I am so hard I can fuck your beautiful mouth and cut off all your excuses."

Reaching out, I undo the top of his jeans and reach for his already hard cock as my other hand pulls down the zipper. For everything I am, this moment makes me unsure of myself, but I force myself to touch the tip of his cock with my tongue. The taste of him fills my mouth, and I suck on the head of his cock while my hand strokes his balls.

"More," he moans above me as he fists his hand in my hair.

My tongue whirls around the soft flesh on the head. Every lash makes his cock grow harder in my mouth. I settle into my task and grip the shaft, letting my hand glide over it. With each stroke I take more of his length into my mouth until my lips graze against his balls. Each stroke is a struggle to breathe until I move back. Over and over I move across his cock and give in to the headiness of giving him control. His hand tightens in my hair and moves my head until he settles into a quick rhythm.

"Are you wet for me?" he asks in a growl of appreciation.

I mumble around his cock, but he doesn't relent. Pressure coils through my core in a clench to match the fist in my hair. Everything in me needs this moment.

"Bloody hell," Reece gasps as he presses deep into my mouth.

His cock pulsates with his climax as his hips thrust and press his cock against the back of my throat. Pleasure sizzles through me, and my heart races.

When he releases me, I pull back and look up. Reece's head is bowed. His chest expands and contracts with his harsh breath. The cords on his neck are taut and his face is flush as his hand presses against his thigh.

"Are you okay?" I ask tentatively.

Reece nods. "Magnificent," he replies and pulls my head forward until it rests against his other leg.

Long moments pass as his breathing returns to normal. The weight of the world evaporates as he holds me in place. Right here is where I want to be.

Above me, Reece drags in a long breath, and a shudder reverberates through his body.

"Help me undress, Atlas. We've both had a long day, and I want to hold you close."

Without another word, I rise and help Reece from his confining garments. Once he's settled into the bed, I lie next to him. His arm drags me next to his chest. For the first time in weeks, I fade with ease into the blessed darkness of sleep.

CHAPTER FIVE

A sunbeam cuts across my eyelids, and I groan. A tension headache claws its way up my skull. I try to force my body to relent and slip back into the darkness, but it refuses. Rolling over, I reach for Reece, but my hand lands hard on the mattress. I open my eyes and stare at the other side of the bed. It is empty, and I shove away the thoughts of being alone. It can't be a dream.

I throw back the covers and walk to the shower. The chaos of thoughts threatens the last vestige of peace, but I shove them away. On the sink, a towel is neatly folded. A packet of pain medicine lies on top and a glass of water sits beside the bundle.

For your headache.
~R

I LET OUT A BREATH I DIDN'T REALIZE I WAS HOLDING.

"He's real, and he's still here," I say out loud and down the medicine along with the water.

The words echo back to me in comforting reassurance, and I step into the shower. Hot water works the tension of knots I do not realize are bunched in my muscles. I push aside any thoughts which threaten to pierce my fragile peace. Until last night, work would give me a place to wash the panic from my world. Hours of mindless tasks and endless decisions would take away the fear and pain which sits on the edge of each breath. Now there are few holds to keep me from falling over the precipice into the abyss.

Dominick's revelations are enough to be my undoing, but there are threads I cannot see. Invisible movements pushing and pulling things into place. It is unnerving. Underneath it all is a game. If I can find the rules, then I can run the game. Right now, this house is at a disadvantage, and that must change.

I step out of the shower and wrap the towel around my body. The lack of schedule both lifts and oppresses me. There is no purpose to my world. Everything was taken from me. They all turned against me, and now I must not only fight my enemy with the Society's Overwatch surveying my every move, but also my friends. Everyone stood in silence as he announced my fate. Anger wells up, and I grab on to it as I step into the bedroom.

The bed is made. On it lies a dress but no undergarments. The last of my emotions break. I pick up the dress and hurl it across the room. Stepping up to my closet, I pull out a pair of dress pants and a blouse, along with a matching bra and panty set. The act of defiance and control takes me off the internal ledge. I get dressed. As I pull my hair back and clip it, raised voices in the kitchen draw my attention. With one final check of my appearance in the mirror, I slip on a pair of four-inch heels and step out of the bedroom.

All around me, chaos erupts. Reece sits at the island bar, his hand rubbing his leg as he argues with Kade. Samantha and Ian stare at a laptop on the island and periodically try to interject in the conversation. Garrett's arms are crossed over his chest, and his jaw is clenched.

In the sitting room, Dominick paces back and forth with his hands behind his back. The tension in the room is so thick a knife would struggle to cut it.

I don't know whether to laugh or scream in frustration. This is one problem I can resolve, and I take a deep breath and step into the room. My heels click across the tile as I head toward the coffee pot.

"Good morning, everyone. I hope you all slept well and are prepared for my normal day," I say, forcing a chipperness into my voice and then plastering a smile on my face.

Silence ripples through the room. I lift my chin and do not waver from my path. Without a doubt, I know every eye in the room is on me. Reece is glaring at me because I am not attired the way he wished. Dominick will stare at me because I do not appear flustered by invasion but will attempt to find chinks in my façade. Samantha is aggravated by her leash to the business, while Ian is unsure if he should apologize about his unintentional takeover. Which leaves Garrett. He doesn't know it yet, but he better be on his game. Edmund is a force, and so am I.

I pull the tap of the nitro brew coffee canister, thankful someone brought it. The dark liquid churns in my glass and reflects my emotions in physical form. Picking up the glass, I raise it to my lips as I turn and face the group. Every single person is staring at me.

"Kade, the health inspector is due in today. There is a leak under the sink and two other problems in the kitchen. You will need to take the hit on the inspection and schedule a re-inspection to ensure we don't lose our permit. Samantha, three major clients are on my schedule for calls this morning. None of their current issues are things of immediate importance. You can reschedule them all if you so choose. Ian, please set up a meeting with me to discuss the change in your investment, as it affects our agreement. Garrett, I'm not sure why you're in this room when Kade is head of my security team and Jessica can give you more information than I can." I pause and take a sip of my coffee. Everything in me is braced, but no one makes a sound. "Dominick, please stop pacing. It is unbecoming. Mutiny doesn't look good on y'all, but please feel free to run amuck at my expense."

I walk past Reece and meet his glare with a smile. "Good morning, Reece. I'm sorry to see your leg is bothering you this morning. Thank you for the headache medicine, it was well-timed," I say and bend to place a kiss on his cheek. Then I turn and walk over to the sitting area. With an air of confidence I don't possess, I lower myself into the chair.

"Please, folks, carry on. It seems my day is clear and I, for one, am curious what an idle day looks like."

I lift my coffee glass to my lips, smile to myself, then take a long sip and wait.

"Atlas," Reece says from behind me. "Mutiny doesn't look good on you either, and neither does smugness. I believe I picked another outfit out for you today."

"Yes," I reply without moving. "However, I did not find it would provide what I needed to face the possible tribulations of the day or the treachery in my presence. I appreciate the attempt to offer me... what it gives, but I'm not sure it is my best course of action."

"Kneel," Dominick and Reece say at the same time. I smirk at their attempts to shift my world and make me listen. This is my realm and my kingdom. One way or another they will all learn this lesson.

"Gentlemen, with the respect due both of you, go pound sand," I say with an air of boredom. "Dominick, you've managed my affairs into the hands of others, who currently seem to struggle under the natural weight of my world. Reece, I adore you, but the world has been heavy in your absence. Yes, I struggle, and more than once I've failed, but I am also stronger for it."

"Survival is not strength," he says from behind me.

"It is if you get to live another day. Edmund has been quiet for weeks now. For all I know he died when he splashed overboard," I say and wave my hand as if it could make the whole thing go away.

Garrett clears his throat. "You're wrong," he says.

I stiffen but focus on making my breath even. "Explain," I demand.

The thud of his footfalls breaks the crackling silence as he walks to my chair. He steps in front of me and hands me a folder. I flip it open and fear wraps around my throat.

"Shall we start again, Atlas?" he asks, and I nod.

THE PICTURES IN THE FOLDER ARE GRUESOME. THE WOMAN IS covered in deep whip marks as she kneels on a rug stained with large dark blotches. Long rivers of blood run trails across her skin. No place on her remains untouched. Beside her, a man hangs with his arms strung behind him. Weights are strapped across his chest. Agony is written in deep creases across his face. On the floor between them is a wineglass with a deep red liquid filled to the rim and flowing down the edge.

The images turn my stomach. I flip to the next one. It is a picture of Edmund kneeling compliantly at the woman's feet. The look on his face is peaceful. It is one I've seen many times. In his right hand is a silver salver with a wineglass.

My stomach churns on the acidity of the coffee. I work to hold my composure and slide the pictures to the back of the stack. The next paper makes me freeze in place.

A,
You could have been mine,
but you chose another.
I hope your affairs are in order.
Soon it will be time to pay for choices.
~E

My hand flies to my mouth, but I refuse to let go of my hard-earned stance. I take a deep breath to settle my nerves. With shaky hands, I shut the folder and hand it back to Garrett. He takes it but doesn't move.

"Who received the note?" I ask as I fold my hands in my lap and stare at them.

"Your security team was alerted to the package by your assistant."

"When?"

Garrett shifts his weight between his feet.

"When?" I repeat the question without looking up.

"Three days ago."

I nod, strangely thankful for the moment of crisis. Here there is no room for emotions. I am past angry, and exhaustion is my new normal. He's finally made a move.

"Have there been any other packages?"

"One. It came in this morning."

Garrett hands me a piece of paper inside a plastic zip-top bag.

Armies gather and in the end only one will survive.
Shall we play a game?

Pick one:
GO
Thermonuclear War

I look forward to your annihilation and the destruction of everything you hold dear.

"WHAT DID I DO TO DESERVE THIS?" I SAY AS MY VOICE CRACKS.

"That one wasn't sent to you," Dominick says.

I lift my head. The look on his face is haunted.

"It was delivered to his brownstone this morning and a second one was delivered here," Garrett adds. "My team is already in motion on both fronts."

"Can we have the room, please?" I ask without taking my eyes off of Dominick.

Why is this happening? I want to scream, but not everyone in this room is privy to the necessary information. Samantha was never invited into the Society. Her need to be free ran counter to the discipline and structure of Dominick's training. Ian, who I always thought would fit in easily, was from the soft world and wouldn't understand. Kade brushed against some members but never learned the actual extent of the organization or the power it wields.

"Atlas." My name is a warning on Reece's lips. Maybe I'm not meant to find happiness or love. Did I anger some divinity when I walked away? I shake my head at the irrational thoughts.

Dominick nods, and papers shuffle behind me. Mumbles of irritation follow footfalls as they go down the stairs. I wait for the tap of a cane across the floor, although I know I won't hear it.

"Reece." His name is a plead on my lips. "I'm sorry."

"For what?" he asks, confusion clouding his voice.

"Mr. Gabriel, if you wouldn't mind joining us over here, we need to read you in on an operation," Garrett says with command efficiency.

"You make it sound like it's a military situation."

"Close, but first you need some background."

CHAPTER SIX

"Why me?" I ask Dominick as Reece makes his way to the couch.

"You know why. The day you walked away, you knew it wouldn't last."

"Everyone can leave. It is the very foundation of it all," I reply, challenging him again.

Dominick looks at me. A thousand things pass between us, but I refuse to give this time.

"Almost everyone can leave."

"And I refused to stay and take the next step."

"It's not something you can refuse."

"I've built a life. I made my own decisions and chose a different path."

"Yes, but a debt is still owed."

"Pick someone else."

Dominick shakes his head and then sits in the chair across from me.

"Someone tell me what the hell is going on here!" Reece demands.

I take a long pull on my coffee. More masks. More secrets. More loss. More pain. How do I tell him all those things?

"Not everything in my life is what it seems," I start.

"I know. You're both Atlas and Alexandra, in addition to a writer. We've moved past the secrets you kept from me, though I never understood why," Reece started.

"More than anything else-I love you, Reece. You are everything to me; you fill a place in my life where I can find refuge and not have to be the pillar of strength and endurance. Since I met you, all I've wanted is for the world to go away. To live a simpler life. For you, I would walk away from much of what I have here."

"But?" Reece adds.

The word hangs in the air.

"Her life isn't hers to give you," Dominick says.

"Last time I checked, we live in a country where our citizens are free to choose their own lives."

Dominick nods. "Mostly."

Reece raises an eyebrow.

"What I am about to tell you will sound far-fetched-unbelievable in some ways. However, I assure you it is the truth."

"Okay," Reece says with hesitation.

"We are a member of an organization called the Sovereign Society. It lives under the layers of the greater human civilizations. We were created when humans realized there were some who lead and others who follow. As time went on, it was codified and contracted. Where the ebbs and flows of the greater society sought to abuse others in servitude for any number of superiority or political views, we maintained something different. We believe both the Dominant and submissive, to use modern terms, are inherently equal in their power. It is by choice, free will, and monetary exchange that the inequity can exist. This, by its very nature, frees us to explore all manner of purpose, pleasure, and activity. It doesn't matter how extreme, we can test the limits of our boundaries or find arranged companionship without the necessity unimportant rituals which waste time and energy."

I hold my breath. Every muscle is tense.

Reece lets out a chuckle, and Dominick frowns.

"You're trying to tell me there's some underground secret organization that deals in human slave trafficking? Every government in the world is trying to put an end to that problem."

"That 'problem' is about abuse and power to fuel material greed. And we do occasionally run into such an issue, but it is dealt with swiftly. Every person enters the Society voluntarily. As such, every one of them can leave at the end of their contracted period."

"I'm confused. You're part of a secret society where people sell themselves into slavery?" Reece asks incredulously.

I cringe at his reaction.

"Everyone in this room, excluding you, is part of the Society."

"Not everyone," I interject.

Reece turns and looks at me. "You're saying this is all real."

I nod. "I'm sorry," I mouth.

"Is Edmund part of the Society?"

"He was," Dominick confirms.

I glance over at Reece. The line of his jaw is tense. He clenches and releases the top of his cane.

"Why is he targeting Atlas?" he asks.

"It's complicated, but I will try to be as succinct as possible. Atlas was trained and chosen by the Society to fill a specific role. She was trained in my house's lineage and under my tutelage; however, she did not finish her step into membership."

"Okay, so she's no longer part of this... Society?"

"Technically," Dominick hedges. "Edmund targeted me because I was the lead judge at his trial, and as such I was an independent voice. I could either follow the ruling of the tribunal council or make my own and pardon him. Based on the information at the time, I ruled to end his membership in our organization and placed him under protective surveillance for a period of no less than ten years."

"Then how the hell is he threatening you now?"

"There was a hole in our security. He changed his name and moved to the East Coast, reinventing himself in the process. As to why he is threatening me, not only did I rule against him, but my house holds the honor of training the next North American Regent. It is the equivalent to a regional monarch."

"Congratulations?" Reece says, sarcasm dripping from his tone.

Dominick tips his head in a regal nod.

"This position is tough to fill and has been vacant for almost two years. Such a person must possess a unique duality. They must be a Dominant, able to lead with both an iron fist and a velvet glove, manage a vast amount of activities, and punish or discipline as necessary. Comfortable with human contracts and be judge, jury, and executioner when necessary. Their staff is vast and covers the entire North American territory. Due to the unique qualifications necessary, once a person is chosen, their choice in the matter is revoked."

Reece shrugs. "While a large undertaking, it is the same as any leader in the free, and not so free, world. It sounds like there's not much choice for them, though, in a Society that is based on voluntary servitude."

"True. It is something one is 'born' into when they are identified during their training. They are rigorously tested to ensure they are equally dominant and submissive. Not just in deed, but in a deep and true desire. They are signed into a contract with a Consort. This person counsels them, pushes them, punishes and absolves their actions in every way necessary. Without such, they can get lost when things around them get complicated. They are the refuge in the storm and the person who can lift the weight of the world from their shoulders. An identified Regent is trained in both ways."

"What does this have to do with Atlas? She's not part of the Society, and if I'm following all of this, is thus not part of your House. Is she getting caught in the crossfire of your stupid games?"

"Don't." The word is out before I can stop it.

Dominick's look strikes through my defenses, and I realize my foolishness when I walked away.

Reece ping pongs between Dominick and me.

"It has nothing to do with me, Reece. I am caught in the crossfire of the Society's politics. Edmund targeted me because he was trying to hurt Dominick. There's a deep bond between a trainer and a trainee. Edmund knew if he married me, I would no longer be eligible to complete my membership in the Society because the outer world and inner world cannot mix on an intimate level. He also knew my death would strike a blow to a very old House. Everything else in my world was of no consequence to him," I say without taking my eyes off of Dominick.

"Omission is still a lie, Atlas."

"No, it is a lack of information."

"Except when it changes the fundamental concepts necessary for understanding and decision-making. Will you tell him or shall I?" Dominick challenges.

Reece bangs his cane against the floor. Immediately, I turn and look in his direction.

"Children, that's enough," he says in exasperation and rubs a hand across his leg. "I will ask once and in that moment, you will both give me the piece I'm missing."

I glance over at Dominick, and a smile curls around the edge of his mouth. He looks over at Garrett with a regal nod. Without a word, Garrett offers a thick manila envelope to Reece. I recognize the seal and shake my head.

Dominick nods, and I turn to face Reece.

Reece weighs the envelope and then breaks the wax seal. He slides the papers out of the envelope.

"Stop. Please," I whisper.

Reece pauses and lays the bundle on his lap. "What secrets will I find in here?"

My body trembles. "I left. I walked away from everything. Not even my membership mark is complete." The words come out in a rush.

"Atlas," Dominick warns.

"I can't... I'm not."

Dominick sighs. "Reece, this is Garrett. He's with Obsidian Overwatch, and his title is equivalent to Head of the Regent's Guard for North America. Atlas is his charge."

The words hang in the air. He said everything without saying anything at all.

Reece's gaze burns through me with such an intensity my soul shivers. Fear knots in my stomach, and my heart hammers against my chest.

"That doesn't sound like she left," Reece says, holding my gaze.

"There are some positions one can't leave," Dominick states.

"Say it, Atlas," Reece demands.

I shake my head. The words will make it real, and I refuse to acknowledge it.

"Say it!"

"I'm the chosen Regent!" I say in a rush of emotions.

"What's in this envelope?"

Shame chokes my words. "A contract," I whisper.

"Well..." Reece says and rises from the couch. "I guess this explains why my contract was so trite to you."

"Reece, please," I beg as I watch him walk down the stairs.

The soft click of the door sounds like an explosive bomb to my ears.

"I don't want to be Regent. How many times do I need to say it?"

"The choice is already made," Dominick says. "The only thing left is the Consort contract and rituals."

"Are you not paying attention? The only person who could be my Consort, confessor, and protector just walked out that door because your precious Society can't find someone else to play regional 'queen'! Not to mention I don't want it!" I scream.

"You knew when you signed your training contract," Dominick points out just above a whisper.

"When I signed that contract, I knew it was a possibility. I also knew I was a Dominant, so I couldn't be chosen because I wasn't qualified."

"Atlas, wake up! The problem is you are perfectly qualified, but you are so scared of being weak you can't see your own strength."

CHAPTER SEVEN

"Garrett, talk some sense into him. There has to be someone else in this vast country to take the job," I demand, refusing to admit defeat.

"Atlas, you know your test scores. Besides, the entire Council of Regents and the head of every House in North America voted. We gave you time to live in the soft world because we thought it would benefit you. You've ignored every attempt we've made to bring you back and place you in your rightful position. The clause in your contract was clear. We discussed it for days. If they chose you, it immediately reverted to a lifetime service contract."

"I have a life here."

"Yes, one you built after you ran away because of the vote. I advised the Council then it was a mistake not to bring you back, but they outvoted me. No one expected the sudden death of the Regent. We've been patient."

"And what if I'd married or eloped?" I say in a sudden spark of inspiration.

"We would have annulled it or brought your new husband into our world the hard way," Dominick states matter-of-factly. "Atlas, you act like it's the end of the world. You'll want for nothing and will travel the world."

"I'll be responsible for thousands of lives and I'll never be free," I whisper.

"More free than you are now," Dominick says as he rises from his chair. "Stop acting like this situation is a surprise. You've known it was coming for years. We've all been too soft with you hoping you would honor your duty and your vows. Every person in the North American branch has suffered under the weight of the vacant position. Now your life is in danger. You'll also note, Reece took the contract with him," Dominick points out as he walks to the kitchen.

I glance over to where Reece was sitting. The envelope is gone.

"He hasn't signed the paperwork," I note.

"Actually..."

I turn to face Dominick and raise my eyebrow.

"He signed an NDA before he boarded the plane in Miami."

"So you're the reason he's here and now hates me."

"I'm the reason he's here. It was my hope you'd agree and wouldn't force my hand the way you did. If you weren't so stubborn, we would have brought him into the Society together. He's exactly what you need, now more than ever. I saw it when you were at the brownstone and I told the Council then we were on the cusp of a win as you left for the islands."

He stares off in thought.

"We underestimated Edmund," he states.

"If you thought I'd say yes, then why did you let me leave without protection?"

Dominick looks at Garrett, who watches the scene without a word.

"We didn't. You've never been without protection. Every new crew member on that boat was Society protection. I can assure you, though, your actions have caused great consternation in several teams. You need to learn to trust more," Garrett says.

"The only protection I've had since I... left was Kade and the team he put together."

Garrett nods.

"Tanner, a former member of Kade's military team, was recruited by us shortly after you started the club. He enjoys the benefits of both worlds."

"Wait. You're telling me Tanner is Society?"

"Yes. He alerted us to some unusual activities with a client of yours, and we sent Cassandra in to assess the situation. Based on forward reports, it looked like it was a minor infatuation, and we thought it would be good training for her. So she posed as someone who wanted to learn dominance from you. When you went 'missing,' she gained access to the rest of the club's systems with Tanner's help."

I stare at him. A slow smile pulls across his face.

"We've always been right here. You've only given us the slip once, and I promise you, my Regent, that will never happen again."

There are no words. I am numb as my entire world shifts on its axis.

"WHERE DOES THE NORTH AMERICAN REGENT LIVE, ANYWAY?" I ask, trying to remember the basics of the Sovereign Society's history.

"Anywhere she wants to, my Liège," Dominick says with a tone somewhere between respect and sarcasm.

"Cute," I say and roll my eyes.

"I am here to serve and please," he replies and bows his head.

"What about my club? The PR firm? My books?"

"There's a reason I handed them to the appropriate individuals. Kade is more than capable, with the right encouragement and training, to run the club. It is time for Samantha to settle a bit and lift the load of the PR firm," Dominick states.

"She'll hate that."

"Indeed, but it's good for her. A ghost writer, or a team of them, can write your books if you choose. With Ian owning a controlling interest in the business now, he'll provide the necessary guidance for their success. In addition, the Society can use the club as a soft asset and recruiting grounds."

I rub my temples.

"It's like you've mapped out my life without me."

"Yes. It was my responsibility and my job. My one major regret is that we missed Edmund's intentions. Moreover, we missed who he was and how devastating he could be to our future. When you showed up on my doorstep, the relief that flooded over me is indescribable."

I frown.

"You could have fooled me," I reply with disdain.

"Good. It was exactly what you needed. You were named to perfection. Without a doubt you can lift worlds, but more importantly, you inspire loyalty in a way that is hard to come by. You innately understand the desires of both Dominants and those who serve or submit. Those things can't be taught at the level you've achieved. I've read your training manuals. They provide an insight which goes to the core of why we are the way we are. Atlas, I wish you could see it, but you are perfect for this position. I've known it for a long time. In some ways I wish I could lift this burden from your shoulders, but then I realize you can perfectly lift it yourself. It would be a disservice to the Society to allow you to walk away," Dominick says. "Garrett, I leave her in your keeping. There's business I must attend."

Garrett gives Dominick a slight bow.

"Take some time to get settled into your new world, Atlas. Time grows short," he says and walks down the stairs.

"Is there anything I can get you?" Garrett asks once we are alone.

"A whip, a boy, and a whipping post?" I say, letting sarcasm drip off of each word.

"Are you sure the boy is needed?" he shoots back.

"What are you implying?"

"It's not an implication. Your world is shifting faster than you can move. I know it must be hard. Maybe your strength doesn't lie in your dominance in this case. The willow doesn't break in the wind because it can bend. Such a lesson might be crucial in stormy weather."

I shake my head. "That option may no longer be available," I say with a sigh.

"If I may be so bold, Regent."

"Stop calling me that!"

"You need to get used to hearing it, at least in private," Garrett says. "Reece loves you. It may be hard to believe right now, but when his emotions settle, you'll realize you are his sun and moon."

"He didn't sign up for this. Hell, I accidentally signed up for it."

Garrett shakes his head. "You do nothing accidentally. Youth may have not given you enough experience to understand the full implications of your decision, but there was nothing accidental when you placed your name on the signature line."

"They should have picked someone else," I say with a whine.

"Stop it. Now. This is where we are, and you will accept it. The Council of Regents may be willing to coddle you, but I am not. Get over it. My teams put their lives on the line to protect you. You will respect that sacrifice by accepting your path. No more questions. It will work out as it should."

"Has anyone told you that you're bossy?" I ask.

Garrett smiles. "Tess says it when she's acting out."

"She's right."

"As you say, my Regent."

"Maybe she should take my place," I mumble as I rise to pace.

"She can't. Tess isn't qualified. Nor is she yet a Society member."

I spin on my heels and face him.

"Don't. We all have our secrets."

I scowl and Garrett tips forward in a light bow.

"Please forgive me, my Regent. As you know, not everything in life can be adopted in perfect order--or at times at all. Unlike you, we live under the voluntary subjugation of the system. While I've chosen a lifelong commitment and worked to get my present rank, I've also found my heart drawn to one from both worlds. They each bring a unique perspective to my life and the lives of each other. It is a profound privilege."

"Why not bring her into the world you so aptly demand I return to?"

"Because she would lose the perspective, and she is well-adjusted to the ebb and flow of modern life."

"You think me different?"

"I do," Garrett confirms. "You recreated a version of the world you left. Smaller but with no less power and control. In it, you work yourself in an attempt to chase an ideal. Here, you seem less happy than before. Somehow, less satisfied. Freedom is nothing if you cannot find happiness in a life full of work nested in a world full of pain."

"You are quite the romantic," I quip.

"And you are lost," he says as he places a box on the coffee table of the sitting area. "Maybe these will help you find your way back again. If it pleases you, I will take my leave, but I will not be far if you should need me."

I stare at the box. Emblazoned on the top of it is the Sovereign Society's Regional Regent Symbol. A key hangs in a lock, its fine gold tassel brushing against the tabletop. With a flick of my hand, I wave to Garrett dismissively without taking my eyes off the box.

The dark mahogany dispatch box shines in the morning light. Across the edge in gold lettering is the word "North American Regent." I hesitate to touch it, not wanting to accept the tangible proof of my situation. My fingers refuse to acquiesce to my demands and move against its smooth surface.

I turn the key and lift the lid. On top is a fine linen envelope. My name stares back at me like an accusation. Picking it up, I slip my finger under the edge of the flap and break the wax seal. No one uses wax seals anymore, I think to myself.

Pulling out the paper tucked inside, I unfold it with care and scan its contents.

The contents in this box are here to remind you of your own words. As the world around us shifts, it is imperative we continue to be a beacon and foundation in an ever evolving world. Your signed contract lies herein to remind you of your duty and commitment. We do not always like the paths upon which our feet are placed, but every person sacrifices something to the greater good. In return, everyone is lifted, and balance is restored. Today, you may not appreciate our actions, but in the future we hope you will look back upon this defining moment with acknowledgment and fondness.

Welcome home, Regent.
The entire North American Council of Regents and Heads of Households

Signatures run across the rest of the page, each one stating its House or area. To see it all on paper overwhelms me, and I set the letter aside as I peek in the box. There, I see several bound books with a sticky note across the plastic cover of the first.

Atlas,
I've had your training essays, notes and other research typed, organized, and bound.

Dominick

I PULL OFF THE STICKY NOTE AND STARE AT THE ONE ON TOP. A simple title greets me. Bound Essays by Atlas Devereaux. Leaning back in my chair, I flip open the book and scan the table of contents.

Personal isolationism and the cost of Freedom in a post-modern Society
Servant Leadership
Service and the Human Social Contract

WITH A SIGH OF RESIGNATION, I TURN TO THE FIRST PAGE AND read words long ago written.

CHAPTER EIGHT

I lean against the windowsill, my arms across my body, and stare out across the grounds. The bright sunny day mocks me as turmoil roils through me. Life is now a series of movements between patches of quicksand. I crave stability and solid ground more than ever. Yet invisible forces push and pull me through each minute.

The soft click of the cane tells me I'm no longer alone. I do not turn. I can't bear to face his anger and disappointment.

"Interesting box," he comments. The couch creaks under his weight. "I guess it's all real then."

"Unfortunately."

He sighs. "I read the contract."

I don't move or turn around. Internally I brace for the onslaught.

"And I've talked to Dominick and Garrett. We should talk about it." His tone is strained but even.

The silence engulfs us as I stubbornly refuse to acknowledge him.

"Atlas, let me be very clear on something. Our dynamic hasn't changed. We've not negotiated anything new since you accepted my terms on the island. Thus, we can do this the easy way or the hard way. It matters not to me."

I turn and face him without unfolding my body. His face is a mask of calm, but tension shifts through his muscles.

"I'm sorry," I say.

Reece shakes his head. "We are past an apology."

"I suppose you're right. Where does that leave us?"

"That depends on you, Atlas. Let's start with--Are there any more secrets?"

"No," I confirm.

"Are you sure? Nothing? Like there's a giant spacecraft roving above us and you've agreed to join them? Or the world is ending in three days? Or this whole place is a house of cards which will fall down if the wind blows?" he says and smiles.

I shake my head and force a smile. "Well, the last one depends on perspective, I suppose."

"Good, because this last one was rather large."

"I didn't think they'd come," I start, but Reece cuts me off. "Bullshit. You aren't that naïve, Atlas. From my discussions, they've been in touch several times. Admit it to yourself at the very least," he retorts.

"My world is here. I have everything I need right here."

"You signed the contract. While I'll give you a nod to your youth at the time when they informed you of their decision, you ran."

"I did no such thing. I carried on with my life right here."

"And ignored their edict."

"Yes, because they could find another person to fill the position."

Reece snorts.

"What?"

"Dominick said you were stubborn, a little impulsive, and often want to deny the obvious when it doesn't suit you," Reece says and gives me a look that nearly sends me to my knees.

"We all have our weakness," I counter in a whisper.

"Indeed. Come here, girl," he says. There's a hesitance in his voice, but there's no question he expects me to follow the inherent command.

I push off from the windowsill and step over toward the couch.

Reece points to the floor between his legs. I pause and stare at the spot. He doesn't move or say a word. The next move is entirely mine.

Straightening my shoulders, I lower myself between his legs. Reece lets out an audible breath and shifts on the couch.

"This position is home. No matter what the rest of the world calls you or the position you hold, I will be your refuge, a place where your confessions are heard and your sins absolved. At any point either of us can request it as a parley or place of rest. Home is where we find our dynamic and where you allow me to lift the world from your shoulders."

My breath catches in my throat.

"Does this mean..." I start.

Reece hands me the Consort Contract. On the top are several sticky notes.

"It means I am willing to renegotiate our terms based on this recent information," Reece replies.

"I thought you would leave me. There was no doubt in my mind when you walked down those stairs it was for good."

"Dominick and Garrett can be very convincing. I've never met two people so devoted to another person and ideal."

I shake my head, refusing to accept his statement.

"They aren't devoted to me, except for the fact they chose me to this position... ideal..."

"There you are wrong. Yes, they want you placed within the Society but only because they honestly believe it will give you your best life and, in turn, a better world."

I grimace at the words.

"Look at me," he says, and I raise my head.

His level gaze bores into my soul and I shrink back.

"We are at a crossroads, Atlas. I've made my decision. Yes, this was a shock. After all we've been through, I thought nothing else about you could surprise me. I consider this a lesson well learned. Now it is up to you to decide how we move from this point."

"Just like that?"

Reece shakes his head. "The decision is made, but it doesn't mean it won't be a long journey," he says as he leans forward and then runs his thumb across my lips. "Every decision you make, every path you choose... you need to know I've got you. It doesn't mean I won't be angry or even insecure, it means we are a team and both of us provide a strength the other lacks."

I shudder at his words.

Reece leans forward and slides his hand up the back of my neck. His fingers wrap my hair into his fist as he leans forward and brushes his lips across my ear.

"This only works if we are who we are to each other. A united front to the world but in private, you are mine."

I nod as his words fill me with trepidation and hope.

"Words."

"Yes, Sir. All of me is yours," I reply, breathless.

"Do you agree to my terms? We can work out the details later."

"Yes, Sir."

"Good. Now that we're back on the same page, it looks like we need to address your disobedience this morning. I remember laying out a beautiful dress for you and here you kneel before me in pants."

"STRIP," REECE COMMANDS, HIS VOICE SOFT WITH AN EDGE underneath it.

I want to hesitate and refuse. He isn't moving us from the main sitting area of the open apartment. In front of me, he settles back against the cushions and gives me the room to move. My body fights against me. The position stiffens muscles and cuts circulation, but I rise to my feet. Without taking my eye off of his, I slip out of my heels and tuck them under the edge of the table. My fingers move down the buttons of my shirt, and I shrug out of it, then fold it neatly and lay it beside him. The button of my pants slips against nervous fingers. On the third attempt to make it cooperate, Reece leans forward and then pushes my hand out of the way. His nimble fingers release the button and push the fabric past my hips. The fabric puddles at my feet, and he leans back once again.

I step out of them and fold them, neatly placing them on top of the blouse. My bra and panties follow in the same manner. When the last piece of fabric folds onto the top of the pile, I shiver in awareness of my open vulnerability.

Reece's eyes rove over my body like a predator looking at his next meal. He takes a deep breath and points to the floor between his feet. A protectiveness descends around us.

"No matter what happens, I will always protect you. When you are in this space, you do not speak unless spoken to directly. Your gaze does not leave me. Am I clear?"

Confusion races through me, chasing the fear down my spine.

"Yes, Sir," I reply and let my eyes drop.

Above me, Reece clears his throat, and I snap my gaze back to him.

"I see this will need some practice. What happens now will be hard. It is less punishment and more a matter of discipline. When you trust my guiding hand to help you lift your worlds, no matter how minor or subtle the detail, we can move together as one. We are more stable internally. Thus, we can exude the power and strength to be what we need to be in our worlds."

"I trust you," I say, trying to force confidence into my tone.

"For both our sakes, I hope you aren't lying to me," he says and raises his hand, motioning towards the stairs. His eyes don't leave mine.

"Do not disobey me on the rules, Atlas. There's a significant difference between punishment and discipline, of this I can assure you," he says as several footfalls echo across the room.

The awareness of my naked form grabs my thoughts. My head turns, and Reece scowls. The shake of his head is so slight I almost miss it. I freeze in position, focusing on him while I try to glean as much information as possible. My breath is shallow, but I work to control its rise and fall. Chairs scrape across the floor. Mumble-whispered conversations hint at both approval and disapproval. I war with myself.

It is an effort to focus on Reece. His approval should be my guiding light, but I know I can take on the world. I am not weak, and yet I am vulnerable. Right here in the midst of a small crowd I cannot see, I am bare before them all. My only protection is the man who stares back at me, his gaze unwavering.

"I see our Regent has found her place. I presume this is to be her Consort," a woman asks from behind me.

"Yes, Ma'am," Garrett replies. "This is Reece Gabriel. Mr. Gabriel, this is the Council of Five."

"My apologies for not rising, but my attentions are necessary elsewhere and in a more important capacity," he says as he lifts his head and looks around the room.

"That is a good start," another man says to my left. "A Major Regent must be comfortable in their duality, and their Consort must reflect the same. Here, Mr. Gabriel, you will rule. A place to give her balance, rest, and absolution, but out there, you will stand behind her, bow to her, and keep her council."

Heavy footsteps land near the kitchen.

"Well done, Mr. Gabriel," Dominick says. "Shall we begin?"

CHAPTER NINE

Reece nods.

"I understand Dr. Dawes briefed you on the basics of the Sovereign Society. What questions can we answer?"

He looks up but doesn't move. I watch the slow rise and fall of his breath and let mine match it. There is a calmness about him that settles me.

"Why Atlas?"

There's a sigh from somewhere in the room.

"Leadership. When one approaches an almost absolute of power, corruption follows. Our collective histories all bestow these tragedies as our heritage. It comes from its absolution. There is no physical expression or acceptance of wrongdoing. When a ruler or dictator is mad, even in the normal course of heated intellectual discourse, they can kill you with a word. We all know power is a heady thing and can creep into every crevice of the mind and emotions. This unnatural imbalance is why many civilizations have risen and fallen."

Reece rubs a hand down his leg and draws my attention. Guilt crawls across me in never-ending waves. Above me, he clears his throat, and I look up to a scowl.

"That," the man to my right says. "The subtlety of your face and acknowledge of a disapproval of action is the difference."

"I'm not sure I follow," he says and turns his head in the voice's direction.

"Here, you hold the power. I'm sure you gave a set of orders and just now she broke one of them. It doesn't matter how big or small the slight, the fact you noticed it now places Atlas in a different position. This push-pull of power in an equitably inequitable arrangement allows for an even distribution. As a Regent Major, Atlas will control a great deal of power and be saddled with its responsibility. It is a heavy burden for anyone. Without a hand on the scales for balance, she could tip either to an extreme power grab or retreat and be unable to control her region."

"What makes you sure I'm the right one? Why not find her a cohort within the Society? Someone well familiar with your customs and rituals? Aren't you taking a chance on an outsider?" Reece asks.

The very idea shoots emotional pain through me. I shake my head at the idea. Without looking down, Reece taps the side of his thigh. I lay my head on the spot. He leans forward and runs his fingers through my hair. I close my eyes and bask in his touch. Right here is where I belong. I don't want to rule, I just want to be.

"You've explained why her particular personality fits your needs, but you've yet to tell me why her specifically? I'm sure there are several people in your vast organization whose traits match these. Either you give specifics, or you can find someone else. If she's going to give you her life, then you will tell me why it is necessary," he demands.

"Atlas," Dominick starts. Reece's hand goes up immediately to stop him.

"I've heard from you and watched your interactions with her. What I want to know is why the other Regent Minors, Submissive Council and Heads of Houses believe it should be her."

"You're direct," the woman behind me says.

"I grew up on the edge of politics. Everyone has an agenda. It is better to know it going in than to be stabbed with it while you're not looking in the right direction."

Another person chuckles. "Her ability to create a fierce loyalty in a short amount of time combined with her compassion and zeal for life drew our attention. When she walked away, she unknowingly sealed her fate. The sheer tenacity to sign a contract, fulfill it just to the line, and make it on her own is worth noting. Some come to us because it is their calling, and we fit their version of happiness. Others come because they want the experience or we're approached by a member. Atlas wrote a paper which could have easily been in our historical archives. When pushed, she explored the concept of human nature and power innately. These things combined are why she's perfect."

"You are right, of course, Mr. Gabriel. We can find another to fill the role, but it will not be the same. If she were to abdicate, we would leave her destitute. Everything she's built would be for naught," the woman adds.

"Is that a threat?"

"No, Mr. Gabriel. It is a promise. Politics is about the greater good and the individual's sacrifice."

The weight of their words settles across the room.

"I see," Reece replies.

"It is a hard position, Mr. Gabriel, but I for one am very glad to see you are considering the possibility," Dominick comments.

A vibration runs down Reece's leg. He reaches his hand in his pocket and silences his phone without comment. Seconds later it repeats the dance, and he turns his watch toward him. A scowl mars his face, but he silences the phone. This time the phone rings with an audible tone.

"My deepest apologies," Reece says and pulls the phone from his pocket. He glances at the screen and draws it to his ear. "Elizabeth, I'm in a..."

He pales and pulls the phone from his ear. With a quick tap of the screen, he leans forward and lays the phone on the coffee table.

"Hello, ladies and gentlemen." Edmund's voice pours through the speakers. "Atlas, I must say, you are beautiful naked and on your knees. Right where you should be. Showing the world your whole self without shame."

I tremble in terror. Reece pulls me closer, but it only heightens my vulnerable state.

"Looks like she fooled me and so many others. No Dominant in their right mind would hit their knees for another person. But doesn't she blush so prettily when all the attention is on her?"

My head snaps up, and I stare at Reece. He nods to someone over my shoulder.

"That's right, Garrett, your precious Regent is in trouble and you're cornered. How are you going to protect her now? I can see everything you do."

Behind me footsteps move across the floor.

"And even if you could save your Regent, could you save the Council too? Which one will you choose? Are five lives worth the sacrifice of one or shall we mourn the Regent's loss in the name of a madman? That is what you all call me these days... right?"

A heavy velvet robe falls across my shoulders and Reece pulls it around to conceal my form.

"Nice touch, Dominick. Prepared as always. You just happen to have the Regent robe with you? How special, but I don't know that she's worthy of that honor. All of you should be ashamed of yourself for following his lead. He's led you all by the nose for his own goals. Just like he sealed my fate with no evidence."

"We've seen the pictures," Dominick says, his voice dismissive and haughty.

Edmund laughs. "Did you now? Well, that was an unexpected twist. I guess I must look back at the tapes to enjoy your reactions. People should know what they are. Self-awareness is lacking on so many levels these days. She wanted to feel the whip across her skin, so I obliged while he watched."

Silence fills the space. No one wants to speak.

"Why?" I force the word out of the desert of my mouth.

"Hello, Atlas," he says with a sneer. "Why did you have to ruin everything when you didn't choose me? Why was my perfect life set ablaze in the humiliation of your security team racing to save you from a question? Why did you choose this loser, whose family is easy to ruin with some well-placed photos and a whispered word? Why do I know your repulsed expression to my questions?"

I struggle to breathe. Nothing makes sense as the quagmire of emotions and thoughts churn through me.

"Why me?" I demand.

"Because it is the one thing this stupid Council got right. You're interesting. Even now, in your most vulnerable state you exude strength. You saw my need for perfection and twisted every word or movement until it sent me over the edge in bliss."

"Then let's both step away from this," I say as I try to smooth out the crack in my tone.

Edmund chuckles. "You don't get it. Either you are mine alone or you perish. I've given you ample opportunity to make your choice, and my patience is at an end. You kneel before someone else in the robes of a Society which kicked me to the curb. I'm glad we've had this chat. Since Mr. Gabriel is so good at following directions, and I'm on speaker phone, you've all received a courtesy warning. What you put out into the world you shall reap seven-fold. That's a religious reference just for you, Dominick. And Garrett, know this, you can't save them both. Someone must be sacrificed."

The phone goes dead and for a long moment, no one moves.

Numb. All I am is numb. I war between fear and furious. Hands help me until I stand. Pins and needles prick through my feet as the circulation returns. Fingers tap my ankle, and I raise my foot. Then it's repeated on the other side. Fabric slides up my legs and fastens at my waist. The robe drops from my shoulders and a shirt is pulled over my head. My arms are moved into the fabric. Flat shoes are forced onto my feet. No words are spoken. Everything refuses to focus.

A soft balaclava engulfs my face. The soft texture causes me to sigh at the luxury until my breath struggles to pull air through the material. Only my eyes remain uncovered, but it doesn't matter; everyone is a blur of activity and movement. A large cape surrounds me, and its hood forces my face into the shadows.

On my lower back, a strong hand balances me.

"We've got you," Reece murmurs against the fabric.

I shake my head. He's already sacrificed too much for me. This is my problem.

"I wasn't asking, Atlas," he says, his voice firmer.

No other words are spoken, but the movement around me takes on an air of precision. Two bodies flank me. Our position and my clothing force me to look at the floor as we shuffle toward the staircase. At the top, we pause.

Below us, Garrett's voice floats up the stairwell.

"Thanks, Samantha. I think she could really use the break," he says, his voice chipper.

Seconds later, hands grip my arms, and we move down the tight stairs in an awkward configuration. When we hit the bottom, I notice the PR firm is quiet. I file the fact away for later as we move through the office. The bottom of the bookcase barely comes into view when the hidden door swings open. My companions change position, and I follow one in through the open doorway. I can hear the footsteps behind me. The lock click booms in the passageway's silence. We move without hurry through the tunnel until we enter Alexandra's dressing room. A bag sits on my vanity.

"Please pack the supplies for your normal transformation," the woman says from behind me. I look up into the mirror to catch a glimpse, but she's out of view. My hands shake as I pick up various makeup palettes and brushes.

"I need a couple of the dark wigs," I say without lifting my head.

Hands place several wigs into the bag. I lay the last of my makeup and other aids next to them.

"We need to move," the woman says as hands zip up the bag. "Not a word once we leave this room."

We move through the door, out of the dressing room, and into the club. Two heartbeats pass before we enter the hallway and continue toward our destination.

Our pace is casual and unhurried. People toss us curious looks. Periodically, someone will smile or give a thumbs-up. With only my eyes visible, I am as anonymous as I always felt. To the outside world, this looks like a scene about to start or already in progress. I marvel at the feeling.

We are halfway through the club when I realize Reece isn't near me. I focus on his words mere moments before: We've got you.

The question is who are the 'we'?

CHAPTER TEN

"We'll take it from here," Kade's voice says from behind me.

My limited vision obscures the movement I hear around me. Several sets of footsteps click, and the cadence changes. It is slower, more methodical.

"Look, Sir." I hear a voice to my right. "It looks like a kidnapping. That would be so much fun!"

"It looks like someone is really in for it," another replies.

Around me, no one acknowledges the comments as we move down the stairs, deeper into the club. As we make the final turn, I smile in recognition. This room is only used by the highest ranking staff. Once it was my apartment; now it is our collective down time space. The beep of the control panel echoes in the hallway.

"There are no cameras or surveillance devices in this hallway or this room. She'll be safe in here until we find out what's going on," Kade says as he pushes open the door.

I want to bristle as he talks around me, referring to me in the third person, but I know he's doing his job while letting his irritation with me vent a bit.

Without a word, I step across the threshold and into the room. It is rare that I come down here, as I don't want the staff to be uncomfortable, and my position doesn't always afford me a close relationship with many of them. These last few weeks have pointed out the flaw in my behavior, but I am in no position to correct it.

I smile as I look around the room. Memories flood through me. To my left, they have updated the small kitchenette since the last time I graced this room. More play equipment has been added, and a large bondage bed sits on a slant in the corner. The once graceful living space is now part break room and part play room.

"Looks like I need to do a club walkabout more often," I say out loud to no one.

"I restocked the kitchenette in the last half an hour, put fresh linens on the bed, and housekeeping did a basic cleaning to the room. I hope the accommodations will suit you, Ma'am," Kade says from behind me.

I turn to face him as I push the hood off my head.

"They are more than adequate. I don't know how you accomplished so much in so little time."

"I had an amazing teacher, who taught me the efficiency of movement and how to use the resources around me," Kade replies with reverence.

"A lesson I think I need to learn based on the mess I've made of things," I quip.

"We all need to return to the basics sometimes, Ma'am. An apology is not nearly enough to express the disappointment I feel in myself in being unable to maintain your standards while you were away."

I shake my head. "You've nothing for which to apologize. Dominick was right. I always hold on too tight and don't develop the surrounding talent. You, and everyone here, deserve my best, and I didn't give it to you."

Kade walks across the room and stands so close I feel his breath on my skin.

"Atlas, I don't know everything that is going on here, but I know this--you are one of the strongest women I know. Whatever is asked of you, you will rise to the occasion. The agreement I made with Ian allows for control of your companies to be returned to you when you are ready to take the helm again. If that day never comes, there are other provisions which are far more positive than Dominick made it sound. He's a prick, but he's always known how to get your attention when necessary. I don't like his methods, though I believe he's right," he says and bends down to place a kiss on my forehead.

"I'm not sure that is true in this case," I reply and look at the floor.

"Chin up, Ma'am. You command an army at your back and a man willing to stand beside you through whatever comes next."

I shake my head. "There are too many secrets I've thrown at him. Each time I think we're done, my closet reveals more than I'd like to show."

"Everyone has secrets and skeletons in their closet. He'll come around. I don't know what you've thrown at him this time, but based on the fact Dominick and his hired muscle is here, it can't be small. If there's anything I can do to help, please let me."

"Thank you, Kade," I say, my voice soft.

"On that note, I will take my leave. Mr. Gabriel will be here shortly, I am sure. He was bombarding the staff with questions when I left him. If you need anything, you know how to reach me."

Without another word, Kade pivots and walks out the door. The click booms in the silence, and for the first time since this mess began, I feel utterly alone.

FOR A LONG MOMENT I STARE AT MYSELF IN THE FULL-LENGTH mirrors across the room. I don't even recognize myself. Where once there was an arrogant lift in my shoulders, now they slouch forward in defeat.

Everyone feels unmoored in life, even though society tells us we should be strong and have our shit together no matter what is thrown at us. Right now, I am not capable of such. I've gone through the motions, but they were only technically proficient. My heart isn't in the businesses. Right now it is like they are stepping stones for the challenge in front of me, but I don't want to take on its mantle. What I want is selfish. To run away from everything and go back to the island with Reece. To live an existence where the world is weightless.

My head drops in resignation. The only path forward is to accept my position. Internally I scream against the challenges it presents. When do I earn the right to stop, to enjoy and to be in life?

I rip apart the clip at my throat and throw the cape at the wall. It lands with a heavy thud as it bounces and falls to the floor. Rage consumes me, and I push over the spanking bench.

"What do you want from me?" I scream to the room.

Everything in me wants to throw things against the wall and revel as they shatter into a thousand pieces, but my control reins it in at the last second. I fall to my knees and sob. Weeks of pent-up frustration let go in a torrent. Alone, there is no shame in my release as I bang my fist against the floor. Each time I think there is nothing left, a new flow of tears streams down my face.

When I am at last spent, I lay my head against the floor and rock until I can find the smallest solace in my tumultuous mood. Without thought, my body pushes forward until I lie prostrate. Every muscle pulls and stretches in the position. Aches radiate from every part of me. My mind runs down each part and realigns my body until it is in the correct position. When I am satisfied, I roll until I am supine, and the process starts again. Then my legs pull over my head. I moan as my breath becomes difficult but do not allow the position to go uncorrected.

Each position in the form proceeds the same way. I pass through fifteen positions until I return to kneeling. Everything in me is spent. My body aches, but there is a calmness. The silence is no longer a weight. I shift one more time until I can cross my legs and let my mind wander.

Visions of Reece dance across my mind, followed by the idea of

Regent in the Society and what it would be like to take my place. I inhale deeply and let the tension release from my body. Here I can more calmly evaluate Dominick's words. There is a logic to his methods even if they were heavy-handed. Somewhere in this chaos there must be an ordered balance. I let out one more shuddered breath and stretch my muscles.

"I want all of you." Reece's voice startles me out of my calm reverie. "Every secret, every fantasy, every dream and ambition. There's not a part of you I don't want to explore, push, or challenge to be better than you are today."

I untangle myself and spin on the floor to face him as he moves toward me.

"You don't understand what you're saying, Reece. The things they are asking of me aren't like a job change. It's a complete change of life."

"You're worth whatever I must change to be with you. I want to be the one you turn to when everything is falling apart and the one who sets you straight when your attitude gives away the level of your stress and pain."

I shake my head. "This is a path I can't ask you to join me on. It's my world to lift."

Reece runs a hand through his hair. "You are the most stubborn woman I've ever met. At every turn you choose to be alone, but this time, it's not your choice. I will be right here, and we will start with your tantrum, though I was very impressed with your submissive position form. You must show me how many of those you know."

"How..." I start, knowing the room contains no audio or visual surveillance.

"I've been standing by the door watching you since Kade left. Your emotions blind you to the world around you, and quite noticeably in recent moments. It is a good place to start our path forward... don't you think?"

Reece pushes off the door frame, leans over, and picks up a bag at his feet. With deliberate steps he makes his way toward me.

"Focus is hard to achieve when our world become unbalanced. As someone who possesses an equal need to dominate the world around her and to submit to a rule where she can shelter, such imbalance is destructive and frustrating. It's like working only one side of a muscle pair. One is strong and becomes the reliant source of strength while the other pushes near atrophy from a lack of use," he says as he moves to stand in front of me.

Our eyes lock, and he drops the bag to the floor in front of me without ever moving his gaze.

"You... are significantly imbalanced. Our time together has only unlocked needs you've too long denied. In it, you've played with fire and gotten burned, but you deny it to everyone around you. Needs once locked tight in your psyche are now running rampant. They are things you can provide for yourself because they are steps to our dance. You might practice all the steps alone, but until the right partner steps in to lead them, they are unfulfilling."

I shift my weight and move to a kneeling crouch, dropping my head to stare at the floor as I start to rise.

"No one told you to rise. I believe you are in the perfect perspective based on your petulance."

His words cut a slice through me. My thoughts battle between defiance and thankful acceptance. I struggle to tame my breath, but it comes in long pants. There's no fear here, but he demands the acceptance of his words.

"Vulnerability is not my strong suit," I reply on an unsteady breath.

"It is because you choose walls. Stepping away instead of stepping in. You want to experience great heights, but you are afraid to fall. It means you're human," he says. His words are steady, and I reach for their strength. "Look around, Atlas. There's nowhere to go but up."

Silence lingers between us. The tension in my shoulders melts at his steadfast presence. I'm not the only one whose world is tilting, and yet he's right here.

"Thank you." The words are more breath than vocalization.

"This will be quite the adventure, my dear. I look forward to learning from those who came before me in your world, as you are lucky to have so many who adore you."

I nod, afraid my words will come out in a choked sob I refuse to release.

"Now, sit. Legs crossed, back straight, hands on your thighs with your palms open upwards," he commands.

The words wash through me and settle the warring imbalance. With a shift of my weight, I lean back and allow my ass to hit the floor. Crossing my legs and inhaling deeply, I allow the positioning to work through the chatter in my mind. Moments later, I shift my hands into the final position and exhale.

"Beautiful," Reece says as the hint of a smile pulls at his lips.

He walks over to the end of the bed and braces his body against it. In my peripheral I see his hand rub down his wounded leg and cringe.

"Reposition and face me," he commands.

I do as he asks and settle back into my previous position once I am facing him again.

"Everything in the bag is the foundation of our path. Together we will work to help you live in both a dominant space and a submissive one simultaneously. Both of us will enjoy the challenges and struggles as you work to maintain this kind of balance. There's nothing easy about this road, for either of us. Here you will bend your knee for me, and in your new position, I will bend it to you. Let me be clear, neither side is greater or less than the other. Each has a need and a place."

I shake my head. "Your words are beautiful, but I don't know if I can take on the mantle of Regent Major," I say to the floor.

"I believe you misunderstand me, Atlas. That path is already decided. We are here to clear up loose ends, resolve the threat on your life, and change your perspective," he says with decisiveness.

His words make me rotate between laughing and crying and back again.

"Your face plays every thought and emotion. I don't know that I noticed it until just now," Reece comments.

I let out a silent laugh and shrug. There's no reason to raise my head. I know the look on his face is somewhere between amusement and displeasure.

"Pull the items from the bag. I want to make sure we are clear on each one, my expectations and their use. Right now, several people are meeting to discuss the Edmund problem. They expect you to appear as Alexandra in the club. I expect you to step into the leadership position foisted upon you with aplomb and grace. Do I make myself clear?"

"Yes, Sir." I force the word through my clenched jaw.

Reaching into the bag, I pull out the stack of its contents. Each one is wrapped like a present that refuses to give away its secrets.

"I give props to your staff. They are inventive, efficient, and can pull together a request like no team I've ever seen. They are a credit to your standards and expectations. Above everything, you should be proud of what you've accomplished here."

"You mean what I've lost here." The words slip unbidden, laced with a bitter tone.

"Watch your tone," Reece warns. "Besides, you've lost nothing. You retain much of your ownership, created a legacy, and are being given a bigger job which will affect hundreds of thousands of people."

"In obscurity."

"It was not my understanding that you sought fame," Reece challenges.

"I don't."

"Then there is no problem, outside your lack of humility."

My head jerks up to fire back a reply, but my mouth lingers open without a sound. We stare at each other.

"How about you take the graceful route here, nod your acceptance and open your... gifts," Reece says.

There are times the better part of valor is to give in and accept the easy way out of a situation. This is one of those times.

I nod my acquiescence, then pick up the package on top of the pile. The long, rectangular box is familiar, and I smile with anticipation. My fingers pull the long ribbon until the bow untangles in a stream, falling to the floor. I pull on the tape holding the paper together until it loosens and eventually joins the ribbon. With a tug, I lift the box lid. Inside, a large fountain pen gleams in the light. The weight of the box hints at its heft, and I smile.

"It's beautiful. I'm unsure how it will help with the aforementioned path, other than signing official ritual documents as most things are electronic these days," I say without taking my eyes off the pen.

"No one thing doth a path make, and thus no one item doth a system create," Reece replies.

I set the pen on the floor beside me and reach for the next item in the pile. I repeat the same steps until my fingers grace the cover of richly decorated spiral bound journal.

"A journal. I haven't written in one of these since..."

"You left Dominick, I suspect. He and I discussed many things. It was his suggestion, and I thought it a good one after a number of other people were helpful in pointing out certain publications."

I frown and place the journal next to the fountain pen. The next item is much larger. With a tug, much less gentle than the previous packages, I rip the paper from around the item. Three books tumble into my lap.

With a shake of my head, I read the titles. Finding the Submissive Within, Submissive Journal Prompts, and Submissive Forms.

"I wrote these," I comment, looking up and tilting my head with irritation.

"Yes. I believe they came from Alexandra's author copy shelf."

"Why would these be in this bag?"

"What better place to start than where you start everyone else?"

I glare at Reece, and he chuckles.

"Now I wonder if I read Dominant not Asshole by the same author if they would be okay with your attitude?"

"You're impossible."

"Thank you," Reece acknowledges. "But I don't think you are done with your packages."

He nods toward the small pile in front of me.

I stare at the last three packages. This is a game I've played with others too many times not to feel the trepidation of what comes next. Knowing Reece spent time with Dominick frightens me and thrills me in a way I would not acknowledge to anyone. Under his training, I felt balanced and unbalanced in equal parts. It was always the challenge and force to push me past my comfort zones which caused this constant state. In it I learned much but thought I was miserable; now, sitting in a perfect perspective, I see his wisdom and reach for the next package.

This time, I do not take care with the wrapping and rip the paper from the package underneath. Seconds later I am holding a shower mounted enema kit.

I groan and hear Reece chuckle in response.

"I will advise you of the routine to use this device. There will be times when you are allowed privacy. It is a reminder that someone else can command your body and cause it both pain and pleasure."

"Sadist," I reply.

"I haven't earned such a title with you yet, my dear, but I intend to do so. I'll have the staff install it for you."

"NO!" I yell. Immediately I take a deep breath to control myself. "It would be an honor to place such a gift in its proper position myself."

"I knew you were clever," Reece quips. "Now finish the rest. We've got other things to which we must attend."

I lift the last two packages and sigh. Seconds later the paper hits the floor and I stare at a medium size butt plug and a pink egg with what appears to be a long tail. "These two toys are most extraordinary. We are blessed to live in an age of technology. They are controlled by my phone, at any distance. I thought it would be comforting to have such a reminder of my power over your body even in the most difficult situations."

"You can't be serious."

"I assure you I am. Quite serious, in fact. You'll also note we're just at the starting point, and I know things will need to be more challenging over time. For those things, I am also several steps ahead. As your Consort, I believe we are an equal match, and now that I am beginning to understand the rules, I look forward to the game."

A shiver races along my spine. Images of meetings with these two toys inserted crosses my mind, and fear rides the edge with pleasure.

"It is up to you to control your mind and never give away what lies beneath, but then again, it is your specialty... Atlas," Reece says as he pushes off the end of the bed frame. "Now go wash those so you are secure in the knowledge of their cleanliness. Then strip and position yourself over the spanking bench you so carelessly shoved over."

My mind is numb as I gather the two items. Pricks and pain run through my legs as I force them to move from their confining position. I focus every effort on calming the rush of anticipation and anxiety.

On stiff legs, I move to the kitchen sink and remove each toy from its package. Behind me I hear the bang of the bench as it is set upright. Reece's moan in response. Then the rustling of objects I can only guess to be the pile left in the middle of the floor.

I focus on the toys in my hand as I imagine the smooth silicone against my body. The challenges which will arise from their use. As if on cue, the pink toy vibrates, and I jump, dropping it into the sink.

"You dally on a task which was quick," Reece says from across the room. "You don't have to imagine how it will feel inside. Finish your task, and I will show you what is in store."

CHAPTER ELEVEN

I do not reply. In one quick motion, I gather up the toys and dry them off before walking over to the spanking bench. I offer the kitchen towel bundle to Reece. Once they are safe in his hands, I set to the task of removing my clothes. My fingers play around the hem of my blouse before moving to the buttons and slipping each one through the fabric.

"Look at me," Reece commands.

My hands continue their job up, but my head moves much slower. I don't want to gaze into his eyes while I lay my body bare in front of him. He grabs my chin and lifts my head, holding it in place.

"That earned you five more," he comments without explanation.

When the last button slips through the top of the blouse, I shrug it off my shoulders. Reece does not remove his hold on my chin. The intensity in his gaze is overwhelming and comforting but unyielding. I reach around to release the hooks of my bra then pull it forward and let it fall to the floor. My hands drop to the waist of my pants and work the fastener loose.

"If you'd obeyed my choice in garments, you would have had no need to strip, though I enjoy watching the ripples of your emotions play across it. One way or another, you'll realize that obedience is a better path but never to a point where it creates the opposite imbalance of what you are experiencing now. I adore all of you, Atlas. Trust me."

His hand drops from my chin and wraps around the back of my neck. He pulls me forward, and my hands fly out. They land in a brace across his chest. Reece leans down, scraping my bottom lip with his teeth before plundering my mouth with an indescribable urgency. His tongue claims every part of my mouth, pushing me to accept the invasion. Pleasure roars through me. This is everything I need, right here in his arms. Lust burns through me until I can think of nothing else.

I lean into the all-consuming kiss, and Reece immediately pulls back, ending the onslaught as quickly as it started. I sway on my feet, dazed and confused. In front of me, Reece works to get his breath under control, and I try to finish removing my clothes. Both of us succeed in our respective tasks after a long moment. My pants and panties fall in a heap around my ankles.

"Over the bench," Reece says with a struggle.

I smile to myself as I turn and face the bench, glad to know I'm not the only one who is struggling with things. As I bend forward and pull my knees up onto the padded rests on either side, the fabric around my ankle falls to the floor.

Reece runs a hand down my spine, and I shiver under its weight.

"It does not bring a Dominant pleasure to punish or discipline the one they adore and love. However, it is the responsibility of such a position to ensure that inward afflictions of failure, unworthiness or a host of other situations are not allowed to blossom into an unbearable weight. To this end, I find you are guilty of being unable to shift into states which serve you better. Lacking the humility, though altruistic in perspective, to lay down the world for your own needs. This creates an intolerable imbalance, one I am sure we will always face and one for which I am the counterweight until you find your balance once again."

Behind me, the rip of condom wrappers fills the silence. The pop of a glove soon follows, along with the sound of lube moving across the nitrile. I mentally brace for his next move.

A finger presses against the ring of my ass, and every muscle tightens.

"You know better. There's no surprise here, since you've cleaned the toys. Relax and make this easier. Either way, it's going in."

With an effort, I force myself to relax, and his finger slides into the pucker of my ass. A groan escapes as he continues to work his finger in and out. Once he's satisfied, the second one adds to the first and starts the process over. Need claws through me, but I work to remain still. When the third finger pushes against the edge, I move my hips to put pressure on my clit.

"Lie still or I'll bind you and add to punishment already earned," Reece says, punctuating it with a shove of fingers.

"Yes, Sir," I grind out.

He continues to work his fingers in and out without hurry until he is satisfied and pulls them from my body. The sounds behind me tell me he's removed one glove and put another on. My brain sits in a pleasure-induced fog when his finger breeches the edge of my soaking pussy.

"Arousal becomes you," he says as he pumps his finger in and out.

The process repeats, but this time I struggle not to move as his fingers push me closer to a consuming climax. His knuckles bend and brush against my G-spot. I push up off the bench, but his other hand slams me back into place.

"Don't you dare come," he growls and pumps his fingers faster.

My fingers dig into the padding of the bench. I hold my breath to find the last semblance of control, only to have it come in pants when I release it. He pulls his fingers out with an unexpected suddenness. When I think the edge of my brain might return to me, the two toys press simultaneously at the entrance of each opening.

"Who controls the pleasures and pains of this body?" Reece asks.

The words trigger things long forgotten.

"You do, Sir," I say without thought.

"Who controls this amazing mind and how it processes the world?"

"I do, Sir."

"And what controls the vast tumultuous swirl of your emotion which lies between the two?"

"The balance of the body's reaction to the mind's process and the mind's reaction to the body's sensations."

On the last syllable of my reply, he shoves both toys home at the same time. The overwhelming sensations push me right to the edge, but I can't grab the crest.

"Please," I beg in a hoarse whisper.

"You don't deserve pleasure," Reece replies.

In that moment, realization dawns across my addled senses. The questions and responses were from my Society training. Dominick drilled them into me at every moment of pleasure or punishment until I could hold whatever he required for as long as he required it.

"Welcome back to the Society, Atlas. I may have much to learn, but I believe I have a wise mentor, it seems," Reece says.

The toys fill me as my muscles grab and release on the foreign objects. There is no escaping their demands, even as they lie dormant.

"Now, before we are both required in other capacities, I believe we have several other things to address. As a person who prides himself in fairness, I give you the choice... left or right?"

I press my forehead against the padding of the bench. Everything in me hates these games. There's no way to win, and it always results in internal 'what if' questions afterwards.

"I asked a question and expect an answer. In the future, such a delay will result in both being applied."

"Left," I scream without thinking.

"Very well," Reece says. His body moves to the side of the spanking bench, and he places one hand against my lower back.

"For an ungracious attitude, I find you guilty by your own admission. The punishment is deemed to be five swats across the ass without a warm-up."

My body braces even though I know relaxing the muscles is better. My mind races at his words and tries to find all the possible discretions I'm about to face.

His hand comes down hard on my left ass cheek. Muscles squeeze against the plug in my ass, and I cry out.

"Count," he commands.

"One, Sir."

Before the last sound leaves my mouth, the next swat slams against my right cheek. Pain radiates in waves.

"Two, Sir."

The next lands across the crease of my ass, and I realize sitting will be uncomfortable.

"Three, Sir," I cry out as the next stroke lands in the same place on the other ass cheek.

"Four, Sir."

The final one comes up between my legs and lands across the lips of my pussy as pain and pleasure war. One fades into the other in an intoxicating ballet.

"For direct disobedience to my choice of clothing for the day, you will receive 10 strokes with my hand in quick succession. You are not to move. Am I clear?"

"Yes, Sir," I say. The words come out of my mouth, but I abhor pain and know the struggle is insurmountable.

His hand comes down fast across the sit spot and continues to rain down. By the fifth one, I can barely hold on to the last of my fleeting composure. When the eighth one slams against my body, I push up against the bench.

Reece lets out a heavy sigh and pushes hard against my shoulder blades until I'm once against positioned against the bench.

"That earned you more. I believe a paddle might bring the necessary incentive," he says. Seconds later, a heavy wood paddle lies against his previous imprints. The coolness of the paddle lies in juxta-position of the pain I know it's about to cause.

When it leaves my skin, I brace. It comes crashing down against my ass with a stroke far softer than his hand, but the weight and bruising of my ass do not care. At the end of each set, Reece pauses and declares another area of improvement. In the end, there were five immediate reasons for discipline since his arrival. Waves of pain carry in a shudder through my body. Each stroke adds to the last until I can no longer count. Tears form on the edge of my eyes, but even they refuse to allow a release. As the last stroke resonates through my body, I breathe a sigh of relief at its end and frustration at my inability to let go.

His arms wrap around me.

"Kneel on the floor, Atlas." He whispers the command against my ear.

New aches rush across my body as I move. With an effort, I slither off the bench and onto the floor. I work to arrange my heels, so they do not push against the angry skin, but it is an exercise in futility.

"Legs spread wide," he says as he pulls a chair to sit in front of me. "Humility and humiliation come from the same root. Here, you will begin your journey to one through the actions of the other. Place your hand on your pussy and let your fingers stroke along your clit. Do not make yourself come. I want you to transform the humiliation you feel into power, so that through your own humility you will grow in greater self-empowerment."

This isn't the first time I've been placed in such a position, but going back to the basics always makes things more poignant and clearer.

My fingers graze across the skin, and the bundle of nerves alights in pleasure. With each pass I add more pressure until the edge of an orgasm is almost palpable. Without warning, the two toys buried deep inside me vibrate and rapidly accelerate my carefully planned path. My hips press forward, begging for release and more pressure. I allow my fingers to slow in an effort to balance the increasing demands of the plug and bullet.

"Don't stop moving your fingers, Atlas," Reece says above me.

"Please," I beg softly as my fingers move to obey him.

"Now, imagine being taken to the edge and left there. Moments later, you sit in front of a conference room full of people where you must lead them in a discussion of a solution. Periodically, one toy or the other vibrates deep within you, but you must concentrate and focus. You cannot come in such a situation or you risk losing respect and position. You breathe through each wave until you find a pattern and settle into it. When you are confident you can relax and brace in a defined rhythm, both toys will alight, and the whole situation starts over. Each time you think you are winning, something will change," Reece says.

"I couldn't... I can't... please... please..." I cry out.

A sudden knock on the door startles me, and I stop. My head lifts, and I stare at Reece.

"I didn't tell you to stop," he says as his hand slams against my inner thigh.

My fingers return to their ministrations, and I bite my lip in an effort to stifle a moan.

"Sir, Ma'am..." the voice says through the door. "You're needed in the conference room in twenty minutes."

"Thank you," Reece calls out without taking his eyes off of me.

Both toys stop their movement, and Reece grabs my wrist. He brings it up to his mouth and sucks across each finger. When he's done, he places my hand back on the top of my thigh.

"Looks like we're about to find out how well you'll survive," he says and moves to stand. "You've got twenty minutes to be impeccably presentable as Alexandra. Go."

My body refuses to move, and my brain struggles to rise from the soft submissive head space.

"Atlas, move. Time is ticking, and I expect you to move seamlessly from one space to another. I know it's a challenge. You need to climb, and I don't care if you don't make it, but I care that you externally look like you are expected to appear," Reece says, holding out his hand. I place mine in his, and he helps me stand.

With a deep inhale, I take the first step and walk toward the bundles of Alexandra's outfits and makeup. My eyes glance across the jumbled mess and work to sort a plan.

"Can you set a timer for me, please?" I ask without looking back toward Reece.

"Certainly," he replies, and I hear the beep of his phone as he presses the screen.

I need to get covered and reach for the standard undergarments. Picking up the silk stockings, I perch on the edge of a chair, scrunch them down, and place my toe against the seam. Then, careful not to rip the delicate silk, I pull it up along my leg and repeat the same steps on the other one. When both stockings are in place, I grab my panties and step a foot inside.

"No underwear," Reece calls from across the room. "I want you to live in both worlds at once. To know underneath your dominant outer appearance that you are also my submissive."

"I can't. It's too much."

"Is it really? Don't play innocent with me, Alexandra. You are either capable of great feats or you're a failure before you walk out the door."

His words hit the right spot, and I step out of the delicate panties. Reaching for the garter belt, I step in and slide it to my hips, then fasten the stockings to each ribbon. Next, I pull on the pants to a meticulously pressed suit and follow it with a bra coordinated to the garter belt, a plain white camisole and waist cincher.

The armor of the clothes increases my confidence with each layer, and I breathe a sigh of relief as I work to apply the trans formative makeup. With each highlight and contour, my face changes in the mirror. I finish the look with a dark red lipstick and highlights on the pout of my lips.

"You have five minutes left," Reece calls out from his observation post across the room.

I pull the hair cap over my hair and wrap it with a wig band. In a final flourish, I fasten the wig clips under the band, spray the edges into place, and work the wig brush to tame the strays. Satisfied with the image staring back at me, I grab the suit jacket and pull it on as I slip my feet into the four-inch stiletto heels.

"Remarkable," Reece says as he moves toward me. "No wonder I didn't know the two of you were the same. If I hadn't watched the transformation myself, I don't think I would have believed your talent for changing your appearance."

I shove the flipper into my mouth to change the appearance of my front teeth and flash Reece a smile.

"False teeth. Really?"

I nod.

"My accent has slipped recently. This ensures I slow down and pay attention to my words, darlin'," I say in an exaggerated Southern accent and flash him a smile.

"You are stunning, Alexandra," he says as he steps forward.

The plug in my ass jumps to life, and I stumble forward.

"But Atlas is amazing on her knees. The two of you together is an explosive combination when you find the balance."

The plug doesn't let up, and I struggle to stand upright.

"You can do this. Find your balance," Reece coaches.

I shake my head. "I can't. It's too much. I can't move between those two spaces that quickly," I pant as the edge of a plead laces my tone.

"Then it's time you challenge yourself to learn," he whispers against my ear.

The bang on the door startles me, but Reece pulls me into him.

"Showtime, Alexandra," he says and plants a kiss on my forehead before releasing me.

He walks to the door in a steady gait; as he reaches for the handle, he turns and flashes a sadistic smile.

Both toys roar to life on a high setting. I grab for the back of the chair and brace for the orgasm as the edge races through my body. As the door handle clicks, the vibrations die. I am left panting and in need. There's just enough time to rise to my full height before the door swings open.

"Good evening, Ma'am," Kade calls from the hallway. "Dominick asked that I am to retrieve you."

"Shall we?" Reece says with a smirk.

CHAPTER TWELVE

Taking a deep inhale, I pull hard on the seam of the jacket to boost my confidence and ensure my attire is crisp. Internally, I evaluate every part then lift my chin and take a step forward. The click of my heels echoes around the room, and I see Kade's head drop in a respectful nod. This small gesture is the handhold I need to climb back to the dominant space this look requires.

With each step, I settle a little more. By the time I step into the hall, the thin façade is firmly in place, but its fragility is obvious, even if only to me.

"Hello, Thomas." I address Kade with a more formal tone which speaks volumes between us.

A smirk plays across the edges of his mouth.

"Ma'am," he replies. "They are assembled in the smaller classroom. The staff arranged it in the style of a conference room by utilizing the extra formal dining table we use for formal holiday dinners and such. In the back, refreshments are being rotated every hour as is deemed necessary. Audio-visual connection is live, and Tanner is providing any necessary technical support while doubling as external security by standing watch outside the door. The tension in the room is significant, and they will allow none of the staff, including myself and Samantha, into the room during their sessions."

I nod at his brief. His tone is professional with an undertone of worry and curiosity.

"Thank you. You've really come a long way in my absence. I am sorry I left you in such a challenging position," I say and offer him a soft smile.

"Ma'am, when challenges are presented, we can either rise to the occasion by accepting small failures and temporary setbacks, or we can choose not to try. With the latter, we will only ever know defeat without the possibility of great heights. No one could have predicted this path, but here we are, and as a team, we will prevail. As individuals, we will achieve more than any of us thought possible."

I break his gaze. His words worm their way through my thoughts. Then I shake my head.

"Remind me to not allow Dominick, Reece, Garrett, Samantha, and yourself in a room alone without me... ever."

Kade chuckles.

"I am sorry to inform you, it is too late for such an edict. We've already met a couple times, and there are plans for several more sessions to which you are not privy. Besides, while I don't know everything going on here, and that makes me uncomfortable, I trust you, and the meeting of such minds together to discuss you is for your own good."

I snap my head up and glare at him.

"Quite a bold statement, boy," I press.

Kade nods. A thoughtful expression morphs into one of deep caring.

"Indeed it is. No matter what is in front of you, Ma'am- jump. For the good of yourself more than those around you."

My hand comes up and caresses the side of his jaw. We've been together for so long. Through so many scrapes and learning situations. His very nature understands me better than many of those who surround me.

"Thank you."

"You're more than welcome, Ma'am. I am at your service no matter where life takes you," he replies and offers a slight bow.

"Then you'd better get us to the conference room before you incur a wrath you did not earn."

Kade nods and sweeps a wide arc with his arm in the direction of the conference room.

"Shall we?"

I nod and step forward. After two steps, Kade falls in line one step over to my left. On my right, Reece falls into the same place. With a deep inhale to settle the last vestige of my nerves, I step forward and hear their footsteps with mine.

WE WALK THROUGH THE CLUB IN SYNC. I TRY TO STAY conscious of Reece's slower steps with each tap of his cane against the floor.

"Alexandra," a member calls as we emerge from the lower levels.

I turn to the voice, a smile already plastered on my face.

"Parker, how are you?" I ask as I hold out my hand.

He grasps it and returns the smile.

"Good. I'd heard there were Alexandra sightings, but no one could pin you down for any length of time," he says as his eyebrows raise in a question.

"After my recent vacation, there was quite a bit of paperwork to attend to. I'm lucky I have an amazing staff, or I can't even imagine how bad it would have been then."

Parker nods in agreement.

"Kade did an excellent job with the last art show. It came off without a flaw."

"Speaking of which, I understand you've got a new model which has most of your focus."

He chuckles and nods.

"Nothing gets by you," he says without commitment in either direction.

"Indeed. My team keeps me well-informed. How's next quarter's show coming?" I ask, knowing the lingering conversation is necessary and costly.

"Quite well. There are more intense concepts which may push the traditional definition of art."

"Does it evoke an emotional response?" I ask, pushing a little.

"That it does, Alexandra. A fear response but it is an intense emotion."

"Yes. Quite."

"I shall not keep you any longer, as it looks like your entourage is getting impatient with me," he says as his voice drops to a conspiratorial whisper.

I offer him the same smile.

"It's not you. It's most definitely me. They think I might bolt if they don't deliver me to a meeting others think is important."

"Are they right?"

I raise my eyes and look to the ceiling as I think on his question.

"Yes," I reply when I've concluded the answer.

"Then I would say it is an important meeting indeed. I will not be the reason you tarry any longer," Parker says and nods to Kade.

"I look forward to your next art show," I reply as a hand presses lightly on the right side of my lower back.

"May it not disappoint. Until next time, Alexandra, and good luck."

Parker turns on his heel and heads to the bar. The pressure on my back increases until I take the next step and move us in our original direction.

Throughout the club I hear my name called, but it dies on their lips before it is fully formed. I press my lips together to hold back a smile. Behind me, I know Kade is heading off people before they approach. My only conclusion is that Dominick strictly instructed him how I was to be retrieved, and Kade refuses to fail a command at all costs.

Moments later, we arrive at the door to the small classroom. Tanner nods to me as he pulls the door open.

"This is where I leave you," Kade says as he steps around me. "If you need anything, please let Tanner know."

"Thank you, Kade, for everything, and I'm sorry for all of this overboard secrecy-you know how Dominick is about things," I say with a sympathetic smile.

"I trust you. As such, I know that if I had a reason to attend, then I would be invited to do so, but right now, I have a club to run."

I cringe at his last statement. The reminder of losing my world cuts like a hundred razors across my soul. Afraid my voice will betray my emotions, I turn back to the door and walk through. Behind me, the click of Reece's cane follows.

Once I cross the threshold, all conversation ceases, and every person at the table rises to their feet. To the left of the open chair at the head of the table, Dominick moves to a formal parade rest, and the rest of the gathered attendees follow suit.

The weight of the formality hits me like a truck into a wall. For a long moment I stand and look at the people assembled in this room, afraid my legs will give out if I move forward. Around the table, no one moves. Behind me, I hear Reece's cane click as he approaches on my right.

"You've got this, beautiful. Take your place. It's not meant to be easy. Up to this point, it was all business and games. Now you step into the governing of a vast organization. You are capable, and you are mine. Thus, I will be right here when the world gets too heavy and you need solace. Now... stop hesitating and take the place for which you were chosen," he whispers against my ear.

When the last word floats across my skin, he steps back.

I swallow hard and take a deep breath.

"Good evening. I understand you summoned me based on the

fact you have completed plans and conclusions about next steps," I say with a confident conclusion I don't know.

Projecting control, I step off and walk to the head of the table. Reece follows at a much slower pace until he stands behind the chair to my right. I take in the sight before me. No one moves or looks toward me. Their eyes are fixed on spots in front of them, and their bodies hold in a rigid stance. I revel in the control and power. It lets me find the next handhold as I climb my way internally back to a dominant head space.

I allow a smile to spread across my face before schooling my emotions once again as I pull my chair away from the table and sit. To my right, Reece follows suit. No one else moves, and I look up at Dominick. Until he sits down, no one else is relieved. There's an open hierarchy here. Reece is right; this is different in every way. Everything in me wants to command Dominick to move, but I know it's a power play. Either I establish my ability to war with patience or I let him gain the upper hand.

Minutes tick by, but I don't say a word, nor do I fidget in my chair. When I think I can take no more, Dominick breaks position, pulls out his own chair, and sits down on my left. Around the room, there is a cacophony of chairs and bodies repositioning. Once the last person is settled, I let my gaze reach each person's face as they turn toward me.

"You'll forgive me for a lack of protocol and ritual," I start. "Based on current situations, time is of the essence and lives are possibly at stake. What are our next moves?"

"Regent Major, if you will forgive us," Dominick starts. His words belie the challenge in his tone. "We were discussing the expertise of Dr. Hart prior to your arrival. We lack a unanimous agreement on any level of such inclusion in our discussion."

"Why Dr. Hart?" I ask and turn my head toward Dominick.

"It is my understanding her background and expertise may provide the insight we cannot gain otherwise."

"Then what is the problem?"

"Society members are cautious to include anyone outside of those who need knowledge of our existence. It is inconclusive if Dr. Hart falls into that category."

"I see," I reply. "Is this the only issue of her inclusion into the discussion where my life is in danger as is the whole of the Society's notice? It seems to me, for those who want to live on such an interesting edge, you are willing to play with the lives of others as long as it does not affect you directly."

"Careful," Dominick growls from beside me.

I clench my jaw before continuing.

"Speaking from recent experience, I could easily conclude you all hope that such a threat will take me out, but why I can't quite fathom. Politics are such an ugly thing... messy business. Which means each of you bring to the table your own personal agenda. With that in mind, let me be clear-my life is my personal agenda. The office into which I've been coerced and forced is not my personal agenda. Making sure our organization as a whole is consensual is my personal agenda. Based on these, there are times we need to reach out to specific expertise. Can anyone here provide a Sovereign Society substitute?"

The room is silent except for the chairs that slide as those around the table fidget. Beside me, I know Dominick's glare is drilling a hole through my skull.

"If you are going to take on this mantle, then you need to learn to abide by the rituals and protocols of this organization. Consort, you need to learn to control this Regent," an older man says from the other end of the table on the right.

Without control, I laugh out loud. The entire assembly turns to me in unison.

"You misunderstand me. I didn't say I didn't know the protocols and rituals; I only asked forgiveness for a lack of them," I say as I rise from my chair.

Around me, the entire assembly rushes to meet my stance and returns to their formal positions.

"Second, if I were a man you'd not speak to me in such a manner. Nowhere in the rules, rites, or rituals is a man required to take on a Consort of any type, nor are they required to be fully balanced between their two halves. Thus, one could conclude you are dumb enough to believe a woman cannot hold this position alone or smart enough to realize that it is better when such a balance is achieved. For now, I'll presume the latter and give you the benefit of the doubt, but rest assured it is something which I will discuss with the Regent Council," I challenge.

The rush of power flushes through me. I grab for it and let it settle over me.

"That's enough. We've got more immediate things to discuss," Dominick's firm voice rings out.

"Careful, my counsel," I warn back and turn toward Dominick.

On cue, the plug in my ass begins to vibrate. Every muscle in my body goes rigid as I fight to keep the hard-won head space.

"Regent Major," Dominick says, his voice softening as a hint of a knowing smile plays around the edge of his mouth. "Everyone is tense. A multitude of situations are causing unexpected changes for everyone in this room. Each person here is working to find their new normal, as well as keep their chosen Regent safe. You've been heard. I assure you."

He punctuates his last words with a quirk of his eyebrow, and I cringe.

"Now is the time to listen. Would you like us to bring in Dr. Hart to provide expertise?" he continues and turns to the rest of the table. "I am sure every member here knows how to hold their tongue regarding our secrets."

I nod my acknowledgment and work to find calm as I retake my seat.

As soon as my ass hits the chair, the incessant vibration stops, and I look over to Reece, who gives me a simple nod of approval.

"Solomon." Dominick addresses a young man at the other end of the table. "Please tell Tanner, our hosting security, that we'd like to schedule a meeting with Dr. Hart. If it is possible for her to come within the hour, we will cover all of her expenses for re-scheduled appointments and anything else she may deem as appropriate for the immediate interruption in her life at our pleasure."

"Yes, Sir," the young man replies as he stands and walks to the door.

"Now, until we are cleared for that meeting, there is other business which needs to be discussed, outside the immediate danger to your life, Regent Major," Dominick says as he turns back toward me.

"The floor is yours," I reply with a light nod.

"Thank you. Based on conversations with your chosen Consort, it is the assembled parties' presumption that you will continue the path to formal installment into the position of Regent Major. Thus, we require a formal declaration of your intention by ritual formality before we move forward in your acceptance. Do you thus swear to pledge your life before us now?"

I stare at Dominick. Shortly after the words 'we require a formal declaration,' my mind went blank. His lips move, but they make no sense. I thought I'd have more time. Several meetings to acclimate and adjust. Or even a discussion or two with Dominick. The world around me spins. I am unprepared for even the smallest part of his request. While I didn't lie about knowing the rituals and protocols of such a formal gathering, I won't admit out loud the length of time since I picked up the manuals. It can be measured in years and not days or hours.

Every eye is on me, and the weight of their stares only adds to my insecurity at being able to lift the position, let alone bring honor and duty to it. How can I leave my friends? They are the only family I have left, and all of them will be left behind unless I can get an acceptance by global decree, which is unusual. To join the Society is to leave all you know behind. It is a world unto itself and only on the fringes mixes with the cultures and civilizations which surround it.

The weight on my chest increases with each thought. No one makes a lifetime commitment in a split-second, and here they are asking me to make two. For if I accept the position of Regent Major, then I accept Reece as my Consort. We haven't even talked about it. I shake my head with the slightest movement.

Both toys buried deep within me vibrate at the same time. It is a slow pulse meant to pull at my attention. My head swivels to Reece. Disappointment shows on his face, and in that moment I am a total failure.

He's given me his answer. Everyone's given me their expectations, but no one sat down and asked me. It is like I am expected to walk the path carved before me without question. It doesn't matter that I know the answer. Nor does it matter that everything before me is wondrous and scary, things I revel in at every turn in my life.

I open my mouth without taking my eyes off of Reece.

The next look he gives me will devastate my life, but it is the only piece of control I have even if answering in the positive will give me much more power. Everything in me braces for the denial I am about to utter. Muscles clamp on the toys as they cause my grip on my dominant head space to slip. I want Reece to know how sorry I am for what I am about to say.

With the effort of ten men, I tear my gaze from his and look down the table. Every eye is on me as I rise from my chair. Like a slow-motion film, every member rises and snaps their gaze straight ahead, except one. From the other end of the table, the old man who challenged me smirks as if he knows I will deny my position. There's a victory dancing in his eyes for a long second before he joins the rest.

"My counsel," I start, taking a deep breath to brace myself for the answer.

CHAPTER THIRTEEN

"It is with the understanding of the weight of this position and path, along with the confidence of this counsel that my answer weighs heavy on my tongue," I say as I watch the old man at the other end of the table. His gleeful emotions are barely contained behind the emotional mask required in such formal situations.

There's something about him which piques my interest and causes concern. Why would anyone on this council not want me to accept the position when they've all pushed me hard? The question rolls across my mind.

I shake my head to eradicate the errant thought and focus on the required denial. With a deep breath, I brace as I open my mouth.

"By the power of this council and the path which it lays before me, in formal declaration I must..." I say and close my eyes. "Accept the weight of this mantle."

The words stun me, and my eyes fly open. Every internal alarm screams as I try to comprehend why my mouth refused to obey every other part of me. My gaze immediately lands on the old man at the end of the table. His mouth is agape as he stares back at me, breaking every formal protocol for such an occasion. An odd smirk pulls at the side of my mouth at the immediate victory.

"We accept your formal declaration of acceptance and thus declare you the North American Regent. Regent Council, I present to you your new North America Regent, Atlas Devereaux," Dominick declares.

I paste on a smile, and the room erupts in a loud polite clap, all except the man in the back. We hold one another's glare until the room falls silent.

Everything in me is numb. I scream at myself in loud long screams while I work to maintain an indifferent exterior. At this moment, I am thankful for years of training as a Dominant and my father's poor wisdom. Emotions have no place here. Now that I've made a formal acceptance, it is all about power and control. Let the games begin.

When the room is once again silent, I exercise my first power move as office Regent. Until this moment, I held the office on a tenuous thread; now its weight crashes firmly on my shoulders, and I sit down with as much grace as I can muster. Reece follows my lead and once again takes his seat.

Beside me, Dominick talks as he continues to stand, thus holding the rest of the council on their feet. It is an odd juxtaposition, being seated as the most powerful person in the room while everyone stands over me. I let the thought work through my brain without focusing on any of Dominick's speech.

When he's done, he takes his seat, and everyone follows. He reaches over and covers my hand with his, and I turn to look at him. There's a smile on his face, but his eyes are full of concern. Does he know I was supposed to refuse? Is he disappointed that everything in me wanted those words to come out of my mouth?

"Once this nasty Edmund business is behind us, we shall set a date for your full investiture and installment into the office. Until then, this council will work to hand over the various areas of power to you, in due time, so you are not overwhelmed by the office," he says. His tone is soft, almost gentle as his look of concern grows.

I nod and press my lips together in a pained smile.

"Thank you, my counsel. I have every faith that every member here will garner their support in every way to not only keep me safe during these tumultuous times but also to make this transition seamless to the benefit of the Sovereign Society and all we hold dear," I reply. The words are forced, and I work to hold them steady. Then I pull my hand from his and lift my chin.

"Shall we proceed with the agenda until we know at which point Dr. Hart might join us?"

"As you wish, Regent Major," Dominick says as he sits straighter and leans back in his chair.

———

THE MEETING DRONES ON WITH PROCEDURES, AND I AM GLAD FOR the fact Dominick took the lead. I sit in thoughtful silence, periodically watching the man at the other end of the table. The hands on the clock tick in slow rhythmic cadence like the drip of a Chinese water torture.

"Motion carried," Dominick says beside me.

I nod in response without a clue to what the assemblage agreed.

"Regent Major, with your permission, I would like to call for a recess," Dominick says as he turns toward me.

"Permission granted," I reply but don't move.

Around the room, everyone grows restless. Beside me, Dominick clears his throat. I shake the numbness from my brain and rise. There is an audible sigh around the room as everyone rises with me.

I step away from my chair to allow everyone to leave the table, but I don't stray far. Incoherent thoughts run rampant, and I can't catch a thread long enough to follow it though. Worse, I don't know that I really want to.

A firm hand applies pressure on my lower back, but I do not turn.

Reece's scent envelopes me, and I take a deep breath. His mere touch soothes the edges of my raw emotions.

In front of me, Dominick approaches, and I tense. When he's three steps away, he executes a half bow.

"Regent Major, a moment of your time if you are thus permissive," he says without rising.

"Speak freely, my counsel, as I grow weary of formal language," I reply with a slight shake of my head.

"Correct me if I am mistaken, Atlas," he says as he places an emphasis on my name, "but were you going to refuse this position?"

I open my mouth to deny his accusation and then close it immediately without confirmation or denial.

"You received my formal answer, Dominick. It is all that matters in the records," I reply, but my voice wavers at the end.

"Are you confident you can fulfill your duties at the level expected?" he asks in a low whisper. Over his shoulder, I see the man from the end of the table approach. His interest is fixed on our conversation, and I refuse to give away my reluctance.

"It's been quite an overwhelming few days, my counsel. My reluctance lay not in my ability to perform the office to the level of expectations but in my own transitions. As you know, my named Consort has been through quite the ordeal. In addition, I did not know I was chosen for this weighty position until a handful of hours prior. I believe, in the grand scheme, if this council will grant me the leniency of such crisis situations, not to mention the threat to my life, I will rise to the challenges of the office," I comment, pushing as much confidence as I can through my words.

"It seems, if I might be so bold to interject, Regent Major," the man behind Dominick starts. It almost sounds as if he choked on the title but recovered with a slight bow. "Crisis surrounds you. If you find these burdens so heavy, maybe you should step aside."

"And you are?" I ask without formality.

"The head of the House of Roses. My house has been part of the Sovereign Society since the late sixteen hundreds. We branched out to the Americas in the late seventeen hundreds, and currently I have minor houses around the world. My house is the house presumptive. We are prepared to carry your load should you find it too cumbersome," he says.

"You benefit if I quit."

The informal response catches him off guard, and his face screws up in a mask of confusion and anger.

"I do not intend to insult you, Regent Major. Merely to avail my house to your needs, wants, and desires in service to the Society."

"Indeed. When was the last time your house was chosen to place a Regent Major..." I ask, hoping he will fill in his name.

"One hundred fifty years ago," he spits out.

"Why so long?"

"Careful, Regent Major," he warns. "You may find yourself embroiled in politics before your time. A study of monarchies, most especially female ones, rarely ends well. We all hope for your safety under your current threat. Such is a weighty burden. I'll take my leave and allow your Consort and counsel to attend you."

With a precise pivot, he turns and walks to the other end of the room. All three of us stare after him.

"Who was that?" The question escapes without thought as I watch him walk away.

"Didn't you hear? He the Head of the House of Roses, whatever the hell that means," Reece retorts. "Though I think his roses are small and his just a prick."

I hold back a chuckle.

"Careful, you two," Dominick warns in a low whisper. "Walter Jackson is a conniving man. Most of us ignore his idle threats and grandiose proclamations."

"He reminds me of the Great Lord Domly Doms in the soft world," I quip.

"Yes, but with more power and actual teeth," Dominick replies. "It's not surprising he doesn't like you. He was betting on your refusal or removal. The council blocks his appointment at every turn, but you are the most extreme version of it so far and the highest ranking."

"That's why I was pushed so hard?" I ask with a scowl.

Dominick nods. "The council doesn't particularly care for his methods, philosophy, or training. His house's long-standing within the Society brings him a certain... privilege. However, we work to limit his abilities to do any real damage, including removing people from his house when it is deemed appropriate."

I watch the room in thoughtful silence. Something isn't adding up, and I hate missing details.

"Why didn't you tell me all this before?"

"We can't... sway a Regent Major's decision unduly," Dominick says with a smirk.

"Humph."

Beside me, Reece chuckles, and the two give each other a look I know well. Like boys with their hands in the cookie jar.

Across the room, the door to the hallway opens. The young man sent earlier to retrieve Dr. Hart walks in and picks up a large staff from its leaning spot on the wall, then taps it hard on the floor three times. Around us, the room falls silent, and all eyes turn toward him.

"Regent Council, may I introduce to you, by request, Dr. Hart," he announces as Jillian steps into the room.

She looks around the room and circles her thumb across her forefinger.

"Dr. Hart," I call, and Jillian turns.

Recognition blooms across her face, and I motion her forward toward me. Every person tracks her progress. When she reaches me, I smile and embrace her in a familiar hug.

"I'm so glad you could join us," I say as we separate. "We could use your expertise."

"Anything for you," Jillian says with an unsure smile.

The young man by the door stares at me expectantly. With a nod, he bangs the staff on the floor.

"Reg..." he starts, and I shake my head with a scowl. His lips press together, and he looks at the floor. A second later, he raises his head and stares forward. "Please return to your seats, so we may bring back order."

Around the room, people return to their chairs. Each one stands behind them as Dominick and Reece take their places. To my left, a chair has been placed away from the table but close enough for a nod of honor. I motion Jillian to the chair, and she steps to it.

When she's settled, I take a deep breath and step behind my seat. The next move will be telling, but even in such company, some protocols can't be broken. I place both hands on the back to steady myself and pull the chair back. Once I take my seat, the entire room sits, except Jillian. I turn my head and see her wide-eyed stare, which is accompanied by a look of an open mouth confusion.

"Please have a seat, Dr. Hart," I say with an air of formality and offer her a soft smile. "We are working on the current problem with Edmund Hurter. Based on your background, I think you will be able to provide us insights on the information gathered and these photos."

I pick up a stack of papers from the table and turn to hand them to Jillian. Her face drains of color, and her head shakes back and forth ever so slightly.

"Jillian?" I ask softly. "Are you okay?"

"Could I get a glass of water?" she asks, her voice barely above a whisper.

I click my fingers without looking up.

"Water," Dominick commands.

I hear footsteps move around the room, but my focus is on Jillian.

"Is this a personal or a professional problem, Dr. Hart?" I ask with concern.

"Yes."

"I see."

CHAPTER FOURTEEN

Footsteps echo around the room as Solomon rushes to fulfill the command. A minute later, he's beside Jillian, palm flat with a water glass resting perfectly balanced on it. Jillian picks it up and looks up at the young man with a tight, apologetic smile. Once the water glass is in her grasp, he retreats.

Jillian takes a long pull of water and then puts it down into her lap as she stares at it. Her fingers fidget with the side of the glass, and everything in me wants to comfort her.

"I can do this," she says out loud.

"Take your time," I respond with a whisper. "We are at your service."

With a nod, she looks up and forces a smile. "How can I help?"

I raise an eyebrow in doubt as I stare back at her.

She nods again and looks for a place to put her water glass. Seconds later, the young man offers his hand as a tray. Jillian tilts her head to the side as she places the glass on his hand then turns back toward the table.

I hand her the bundle of papers and photos.

"Be aware, there are some disturbing photos. If this becomes too much for you, we will adjourn and ask for you a recommendation for one of your colleagues."

"Thank you for letting me know," she says as she takes the stack with shaking hands.

As she looks through the papers, there is an occasional rustle or shift around the large table. Emotions run in waves across her face, but I know better than to reach out. When she's done, Jillian piles the papers on her lap and closes her eyes. A moment later, she lets out a deep sigh and rises from the chair.

"Before I begin, I will offer you my disclaimer. The person in this investigation was not only my patient but also attacked me prior to flying to Boston. By the very nature of these things, I have an automatic bias. If this information changes the way you view me and would rather one of my colleagues assist you, then I understand and agree. However, if this bias is not bothersome to this assembly, I am more than willing to give my professional and personal opinion," she says, a quiver in her voice as she works to portray confidence.

I look over at Dominick and raise an eyebrow. With a slight nod, he acknowledges my unspoken question and turns to the rest of the table.

"Are there any objections to Dr. Hart's opinion, recollection of her own events and professional analysis?"

"I think it best we use another professional for this analysis," Walter Jackson says from the other end of the table.

"Objection noted," Dominick says, cutting him off from any further elaboration. "Are there any other objections?"

Whispered comments and conversation sweeps through the room for the next few minutes until it dies into quiet once again.

"As silence is an identified measure of compliance for this assembly, I will take such as no further objections. I'm sorry, Mr. Jackson, but while your objection is noted, it is overruled," Dominick concludes and turns back to me. The nod replaces the normally spoken interaction.

"Thank you, Dominick. Dr. Hart, we can begin at your leisure. Is there anything you need to move forward with your perspective?" I ask.

"Someone needs to let Ian know," Jillian says as she looks to the floor.

"Of course," I say with a nod in Dominick's direction. "Anything else?"

"No. I appreciate your understanding. No better time to slough through the mud of these memories like the present," she says as she looks over to Reece.

FOR THE NEXT THIRTY MINUTES, JILLIAN RELIVES HER nightmare. She talks about her sessions with Edmund and the patient-doctor privilege. It is Edmund's attempt on Reece's life that broke part of that seal, she explains. With each layer she pulls back, the noise in the room rises in whispered conversation and the shift of chairs.

"In my professional opinion, Mr. Hurter is a highly intelligent man whose need for approval and acceptance exceeds the capacity of most relationships. In addition, while his childhood was laced with deep abuse, there was something in his later life which drove him to more vicious acts. It is like he craves the approval of someone and continues to push further. The gentle and charming overtone hints at formal training rivaling that of a finishing school while his background denies the fiscal resources for such attendance. In session, he often tried to manipulate the conversation in an attempt to turn it from him to my personal life or others around him. I realize he'd developed an obsessive fixation on a particular person, but it was not until much later, after the..." she says and looks over at Reece with a sympathetic gaze. "Um... attempted murder... that... um... the situation began to... well, fill out."

All eyes turn toward Reece and me.

"Dr. Hart," I start as I stare back down the table. "Do you believe Edmund was acting of his own volition?"

"I... well, I mean to say..." she stutters. "I don't know. I always thought the escalation of his actions was out of character based on the base diagnosis and given history, but things can make people snap and change their demeanor. While I hold to the idea that he was originally trying to manipulate situations to act out his own fantasies, the extreme escalations make little sense."

"So you think what, Dr. Hart? That someone put him up to this? That seems a little absurd. Based on your own events, he seemed to act alone. On the boat he was alone, according to Mr. Gabriel's own report," a woman says from the middle of the table.

Jillian nods her head. "Yes. The fact he always seemed well-informed never fit into his presented pathology. But then again, from what I've been told, several surveillance bugs were found in the club and the adjacent PR firm during a security sweep. This may explain some of his foreknowledge."

"Was your office swept for bugs, Dr. Hart?" Mr. Jackson asks and levels a dead stare in my direction.

"Excuse me?" Jillian replies as she stares down the table.

"The question was clear," he says as he moves his gaze to her.

"No. A security sweep was never performed on my office."

"Let me get this straight. Surveillance bugs were found in other places where this Mr. Hurter was located, but your office was not checked? Someone did a poor security follow-up. It's no wonder you can't catch this man. The security around here is imbecilic."

"Walter, that's enough," Dominick warns.

I scowl and press my lips into a thin line.

"Dr. Hart, thank you for providing an account of your own events and professional insight. I believe you will find Ian waiting for you outside," I say without looking over to her.

"How?"

The question dies in the room without an answer as the young man steps beside her.

"This way, Dr. Hart," he says and gestures to the door.

The tension in the air is palpable. Fury, disappointment, fear, and several unnamed emotions wrack through me as patterns and conclusion form in my mind. As soon as the door clicks closed behind Jillian, I am on my feet. Around the room, people scramble to follow and stand in the appropriate positions.

"My counsel, please call a recess for today," I say as I close my eyes.

"Yes, Regent Major. Council, you are dismissed, but you remain at the call and service to your Regent in this hour of need."

The weight of his words slams against me and with it the realization that my moment of defiance has cost me my life. For they are not in service to me, but I to them until my last breath.

AROUND US, THE ROOM CLEARS, BUT DOMINICK AND REECE remain in their places. When the last person walks out and the door clicks, I pull out my chair and slump into it. I rub my temples and work to process the patterns which won't quite link.

"I want to see Kade, Garrett, and Ian as soon as possible," I say without looking up.

"It'll wait until morning," Dominick says beside me.

Everything in me tenses. I will not take on the weight of the world only to have my requests denied when I deem them important.

"No. It will not," I growl.

"Atlas," Dominick starts in a low warning, but I pause him with a raise of my hand.

"You forget yourself, my counsel," I say and look up into his stunned face. "Let me try this again. I expect Kade, Garrett, and Ian either in this room or my chambers as soon as it can be arranged."

"You have no chambers, Regent Major. You will always have an office and a private area once we settle you, but the chambers belong to the Consort. Might I advise you to dust off those manuals you refused to read years ago."

I sigh.

"With the respect due, barely, it's been a long day. This morning was not supposed to end like this, and I had no..." I catch myself and let out a long breath.

"Go on, complete the sentence," Dominick coaches.

I shake my head. "It is no matter of importance," I say and wave my hand to make the conversation erase in thin air. "I need the three people because some things in my mind aren't making sense, which I will chalk up to my world tilting on its axis, more than once in recent memory. All I'm asking is that you do your job and set up the meeting."

With a glare, I look up at him and dare him to push me one step further. At that exact second, the butt plug vibrates in my ass, but I refuse to back down. Dominick and I stare at each other for a long, tense moment. With each passing second, another notch of the toy's intensity is ramped. When I refuse to budge, the second one adds its voice to the first. Everything in me works to hold my position. The weight of this world comes with power, and I will not yield it in such a situation. To do so will prove I am an easy puppet, and that opinion will not do for this life sentence.

The edge of an orgasm creeps through my body. The knowledge that Reece is attempting to get my attention does not go unnoticed, and my head space starts to shift. I grit my teeth and don't let my expression change except to become a harder mask. Pushing my chair back, I rise and turn to Dominick. Immediately, he acknowledges me with a half bow.

"As you wish, Regent Major," he says and heads for the door. "Consort, I believe it will be in everyone's best interest if we took time for a discussion."

I turn toward Reece. The last vestige of my control dissipates as he nods to Dominick, and we watch him walk through the door. A soft click reverberates around the room as I lean forward and grab the large table with both hands.

"Please," I force the word through clenched teeth.

"Grace and subtlety are tools a leader must hone well, as well as the hammer in various sizes," Reece says, and both toys die.

I use every ounce of remaining strength to hold my body upright as the edge of the orgasm recedes.

"Power and control are two separate concepts," he continues as the toy in my pussy buzzes at its lowest setting. "One can have power but lack control, and one can have control but lack power."

The toy's insistent vibration ramps. I pant and work to slow down my breathing to find any level of control over my body, but it refuses to obey.

"Here I sit in a chamber with a great deal of power surrounding me while they all vie for control, and yet I am the only one who can accurately wield it at the moment."

His hand curls under my wig and into the base of my hair. The move undoes my head space, and I fight the fall from Dominant to his submissive.

"Not here," I beg.

"Part of being mine is that you are mine anywhere. The dance between us is the fact you are dominant to the rest of the world and must maintain a split perspective without giving yourself away," he says and punctuates his words by turning up the intensity of both toys.

"You see, I've dealt with the likes of the people around this table. Some of them are here because they want to serve the greater good. Others are here for their own political gain or worse, they want to rule their version of the ultimate world. Yet you are the one who sits at the head of this table with all the power in your hands. With it you can elevate them or crush them, and they know it, but you must remember, until you can understand your own control-its master sits at your right hand."

Both toys light up and push me hard toward an orgasm. Reece's hands tighten in my hair, and I lose my grip. Right on the edge, my body pants and pleads. My hips push back toward him of their own volition, but I do nothing to stop them. The edge of the wave starts, and I moan.

Reece kills both toys in an instant. My body lurches forward onto the top of the table for support as the orgasm dies on the edge in a ruined state. I want to scream. I want to curse. I want to fall to my knees and beg him to make me his.

"Now get yourself together. Jillian will need Ian tonight after her analysis today. Besides, your meeting can wait until tomorrow. This day did not turn out as either of us expected. I think it is best we turn in and start fresh tomorrow," Reece states as he releases his hold on my hair and steps away from me.

I don't move. My mind is a jumble of thoughts, and I don't want to know the disarray of my physical appearance. With each deep breath, I find a little more control until I push off the table and stand before Reece.

"You are a beautiful, amazing woman. First rule, never forget that or your own power. Second rule, I will always grab control when you fail to wield the first rule with grace and poise because it is what I expect from you. This is what you experienced today. Not my puppet on a string but a silent reminder of both your place and your power. We... are in this together. No matter where the road leads or the adventures take us."

I shake my head. Regret fills me as I realize my folly not only doomed me but also Reece.

"What if you grow tired of all--" I say, gesturing around the room, "--this?"

"Then I guess I must find ways to amuse myself while challenging you," he says with a smirk. Then he places a finger under my chin and forces me to look into his eyes. "Is this the plan and road map I had for my life or our relationship?"

He shakes his head. "No," he continues, "but it is the hand we've chosen to accept. I didn't plan on getting stabbed in the leg either, but it is our reality."

I cringe and pull back, but he adds his thumb to the grip. With a slight tug on my chin, he pulls me toward him.

"This isn't your fault, Atlas. My injury results from the actions of a madman. He is guilty. You are not. The sooner you accept this fact, the better off we will both be in life."

"I am the reason. He was after me. I put everyone in danger. It doesn't matter why it happened, but you can't deny I am the actual cause," I say, remorse and agony lacing through my words.

Reece sighs. "This is something we need to work through, especially as this cane will be my friend for some time to come. For now, will you at least accept the fact that I, personally, hold you blameless?"

I shake my head.

"Atlas," he warns.

"I can accept the fact it is a belief you hold, no matter my opinion on the matter. It is as much as I can offer right now."

Reece nods and leans forward to kiss me on the forehead.

"Fair. We'll get you there. For now, let's get you back to the Consort's chamber and see how you do with incessant vibrations and sleep."

"You wouldn't dare," I accuse.

He chuckles in response and holds out his elbow. "Shall we, Regent Major?"

I smile and take his arm.

"As you wish, my Consort," I say as we start toward the door. "But really? The Consort owns the chambers? What if there's a fight? It's not like I can kick you out of your own chambers."

Reece shakes his head in amusement. "Then I guess you should get used to the floor. Maybe I'll invite you into my bed if you've done your job well," he says.

"You can't be serious!"

His only reply is a smile as we step out of the room.

"Tanner, thank you for your time today, but I've got it from here. Please let Dominick know that the request can hold until tomorrow," Reece says.

"I'll convey the message, Sir, but I've been instructed to escort you both back to... well, you know."

"We'll be fine, Tanner. The club is crawling with security, and I'm positive, if I know Kade, the command center is running a full staff twenty-four by seven with so many unexpected on-site guests," I say and offer him a smile.

"You do indeed know him, Ma'am, but he'll have my hide if I don't follow his orders."

"Tell him I overruled you. He can come to me with any concerns," I reply.

"For the record, I don't like it, but I also can't go against you. Especially with the hierarchy around here a little muddy."

"Good, then it's settled. Go do whatever it is you would do if you weren't babysitting this door, and I'll see if I can clear that muddy hierarchy up for you, as well as the rest of the staff."

Tanner smiles. "Much appreciated, Ma'am. Have a good evening," he says and turns to walk toward the command center.

"Take me to your chambers, or lose me forever," I quip as we step off in the direction of the hidden apartment.

CHAPTER FIFTEEN

"Your wish is my command, my liege," Reece says as we step away from the door.

For a few steps we walk in companionable silence, but a jumble of thoughts pull through me.

"In all seriousness, what would happen if we fought? I mean, if I only have an office and a private space then where am I expected to sleep?"

"We both have much to learn about this new situation, but I don't think it will be a problem. It's best if we don't fight before bed anyway, and this arrangement gives a good balance of power. Thus, in theory, making sure that absolute power doesn't corrupt absolutely."

"There's nothing powerful about my position. From my brief interaction with the Council, it appears they don't really want me in the position unless they can control me. The outside appearance makes it look like I hold the keys to the kingdom, but in reality, I have the smallest voice in the room," I say as my eyes drop to the floor.

"Stop. Right there," Reece growls under his breath. "They are all showing their parts and hitting you when they know you are the most vulnerable. Both of us are new to this game, and everyone in that room knows it. Add that to the crisis of their making, and it's a hard situation. Everyone is trying to gain power while it's on the table and lessen their own liability."

I shake my head in frustration. "Or maybe they think I'm weak."

"Keep that up, and you'll prove them right," he hisses.

"Alexandra," a male voice calls from behind us.

Reece stops our forward progress and allows me to move around him and stare at a man walking toward us. Irritation races through me at the interruption from a stranger, but I'm used to being recognized and approached as I walk through the club.

"Please pardon me for the intrusion to your evening, my R..." The word dies on his lips as he remembers his location. On his suit lapel, the Sovereign Society symbol glints in the light. "My name is Jacob White. Dominick thought it might be best if I introduced myself quickly and offer my services should you need them."

"You work with Dr. Hart?" I reply.

Jacob nods as a smile pulls at the edge of his mouth.

"Yes. Jillian and I are friends. I am a forensic hypnotist, among other titles. Dominick said it might be helpful in the investigation to pull details which may be missed after a traumatic event. Or possibly help you both with some PTSD work."

"Does Jillian know?" I say with a nod to his lapel.

"No," he states and raises an eyebrow in question.

"I see."

"Why, if I might inquire, do you ask?"

"I was just wondering how hard it was to live in both worlds," I reply with a smile which is only politeness.

"An odd question. I presumed with your recent title and this club, you were several years into such a situation."

I shake my head and frown. "It's complicated."

"Then you'll find living in both worlds to be the same. Some people do well with the knowledge and others do not. There's a reason the induction process is... difficult, but I'm not telling you anything you don't already know."

I press my lips together in frustration as Reece's hand presses on my lower back.

"My apologies for cutting our conversation short, Dr. White, but there are things which need our attention."

"It is I who should apologize for the approach. I thought it better to do so casually and give you a name to a face," he says with a slight bow.

"Thank you. I'd like to sit down and talk about some things. Can you please get with Dominick and set some time on my calendar? He's acting as my secretary until such a time we can find the appropriate candidate."

"Of course. I look forward to our discussion," he replies and then with a graceful turn heads back into the main club.

"I've got to get some control over my person and time," I say as I look up at the ceiling.

Reece chuckles beside me.

"What?" I demand.

"You'll find those things difficult for a while. The top of the food chain isn't what it appears in fairy tales and movies."

"I'm queen of the world!" I say as I skip out of his reach. "And I'm taking over the Consort chamber as my own. Since it is in my club."

I laugh as I slip out of his grip and head down the hall. Behind me, the click of his cane echoes off the walls.

There will be trouble, but this version will be fun, I think to myself as I press in the security code and open the apartment door.

I step inside and walk over to the kitchen bar as I remove my wig. Pouring a glass of water from the filter pitcher on the bar, I take a long pull on the cool liquid.

Behind me, the door slams shut, and the soft click of the lock punctuates the silence.

"You move faster than I thought," I say to Reece and turn to face him.

"Good evening, Atlas," Edmund says as he leans against the door.

Fear pours through me as an acrid taste fills my mouth.

"What the hell are you doing here, Edmund?" I say, but my tongue is heavy.

"Women," he says, shaking his head. "My mentor always said that women in power were actually weak. It was the men who controlled the kingdom even if the woman wore the crown for the public. Is that true, Regent Major?"

With each word, he stalks closer, and I back up until I stumble against the kitchen bar.

"How?" I force the word out of my mouth as my muscles start to go slack.

"I have friends in high and low places, Atlas. Some of them don't like you, and others are easily paid with the right sum of money. Here I thought our time together would be difficult, what with your Consort always around and a constant security guard with you. Yet here you are, all alone."

My legs buckle under me, and Edmund reaches out to catch me. Without effort, he spins me until my back slams against his chest and his arm holds me in place around the waist. I fight the spin of the room and refuse to let my body collapse. The sharp edge of a knife presses against my chin and forces my head back onto his shoulder.

"Atlas." Reece knocks on the door. "Open this door or there will be trouble."

"Not a word," Edmund hisses against my ear as the blade presses into my skin. "Unless you want to join your boyfriend in the invalid club."

My breath comes in hard pants. Every muscle in my body refuses to obey my internal commands. Panic flushes through me. I try to calculate how fast help will get here, but I know a single flick of his wrist can end my life.

"Atlas!" Reece screams my name as he bangs on the door.

"If you value your life and the life of your Consort, you'll tell the Council tomorrow you've made a mistake and abdicate. Make up something about how you love your club and friends. I don't actually care what you tell them, as long as the abdication papers are on the table by the end of the day."

He slips the knife up the center of my blouse, slicing the fabric with ease.

"Nnnn... ooo." I fight to voice the refusal.

"It's sharp. Your skin is less resistive than the fabric, I assure you."

He pushes me forward just enough to pull the blouse off my shoulders until it is low enough to bind my arms behind me then pulls me back in place against him.

Edmund laughs as I struggle.

In the next instant, pain screams across my skin as the knife slices a line across my collarbone. The warmth of blood oozes across my skin.

"Ppp... llleeaassee," I try to plead.

"That's right, beg me. I've always loved blood play," he says as the tip of the knife presses into the hollow of my throat. "Do it with a knife and your bottom doesn't know if you'll let the blade kiss the skin or if your mark will dig deep into an everlasting scar. But I assure you, my dear, you'll never rid yourself of my mark."

"ATLAS!" Reece screams.

"Looks like I'm about to run out of time," Edmund says as the knife pulls against my skin in a hard line from the hollow of my neck until the point presses hard between my breasts. "Last time I left Reece a little token to remember me; this time it's your turn. You were supposed to be mine. It would get you out of the way, let the proper leaders lead our organization into the light, and reward me for a job well done, but you are a tease. You refused the simplest request. It's time you were taught your place. Next time, I shove myself down that pretty little throat of yours."

Three more knife strokes create sheer pain as he moves the knife towards my left arm.

A gurgled scream is all I can produce as I try to shake my head in objection.

"Good help is so hard to find when it comes to clean water. A little paralytic, something to increase the sensitivity of the nerves and make you forget every detail," he says as he recuts the last three strokes.

"You can make this end. Abdicate. Endure the Society's punishments. It's all on your shoulders," he says and drops my body to the floor.

"Atlas." Kade's voice joins Reece's from the other side of the door.

"Looks like the cavalry has arrived. Time for me to exit stage left," Edmund says above me. "There's so many things I want to do to you, especially in this state."

He digs his fingers into the cuts and pulls as the warm blood smears across my chest.

"Yyyy.... oooo.. uu--" I shake my head and try to focus on the words, but my eyelids are heavy. Every limb is as heavy as lead.

"Yes, I will win. We always win. This time we will simply be on top when we do," he says and smears his hand across my face as the world fades.

Edmund disappears from above me as the banging on the door becomes more furious.

"Atlas," the male voices demand from the other side.

Time loses meaning as I fight to keep my eyes open. My breath comes in hard pants, and I focus on each one.

The room explodes in a loud crash as the fight drains from me.

"Fuck!" Kade says in the far distance as the cacophony of voices fades into the darkness.

MY EYELIDS REFUSE TO OPEN, NO MATTER HOW MUCH I DEMAND them to listen. Every muscle aches while every nerve ending feels like it is firing off in constant alarm. Voices yell while others growl in harsh tones, but none of their words make sense. My body runs hot and cold in waves, but it refuses to move. My chest moves without effort, but I can't figure out how to draw a breath. I want to tell the noise to stop, but I can't. Then the darkness pulls on me again until silence is my friend.

"SHE SHOULD BE IN A HOSPITAL," A VOICE SAYS FROM somewhere in the room.

"No," a deep male voice responds. "Everything she needs is here, including the medical expertise. I assure you, these people are the finest specialists in the area."

"How do you know?"

"Because they were all vetted for her team," the deep male voice replies. "I know you're upset, but this isn't the time or place."

Somewhere a door opens and closes.

"My team found the problem. Jessica is running deeper backgrounds on the contractors," a familiar voice says, but my brain refuses to place it. "What is his end game?"

The heaviness creeps across my body, and I struggle to focus on the words. They make little sense, but something in me tells me they are important.

"That's complicated."

"Then uncomplicate it, you son of a bitch. This is your fault!" the familiar voice screams as I slip away into the depths of silence.

EVERYTHING IS SILENT EXCEPT THE INCESSANT BEEPS OF machines and the sound of an air pump. I try to catch my breath, but something refuses to let me. Panic rips through me, and I try to struggle. In my mind I scream, but it refuses to leave my body. Not even my eyes will open. Beside me, the beeping gets faster as I struggle to catch a breath.

"Atlas." A female voice demands my attention. "Don't struggle.

You're on a ventilator, and if you work against it, then you'll hurt yourself. This should help."

Warmth creeps up my arm and through my body. With each second, the panic subsides a little, and the beeps slow down.

"You're safe," the female voice continues. "Let your body rest a bit more. All the drugs are almost gone."

I try to shake my head, but my body won't move. The warmth envelopes me like a hug, and I give in once again.

"SOME OF THE COUNCIL ARE DISCUSSING HER ABDICATION," THE deep male voice says in a gruff whisper.

"Cowards," a different familiar voice adds. "We created this monster. They can't blame it on her. She's done nothing wrong."

"She's done plenty wrong, Garrett. I appreciate your loyalty and protectiveness, but you need to recognize her mistakes or you can't teach her. You must demand that she does better, and change your own protective detail team strategies to accommodate when she doesn't."

The man he called Garrett sighs.

"Where's Reece?" he asks.

"The doctor gave him a sedative. He's been by her side for the last four days, and his sleep deprivation was doing none of us any good."

"He's worried about her."

"I know. We all are, but he can't blame himself. Edmund's getting sloppy or someone wanted her dead. I don't know which one. This cocktail almost killed her. The paralytic was far too strong."

"I just hope she remembers something useful."

"Me too."

What am I supposed to remember? I try to scream. The monitor speeds up, and I fight against the ventilator to talk.

"Atlas." The gruff voice calls my name. "Calm down. I know this is hard, but stop fighting. Let your body heal."

I push harder and work to hold my breath, but the air forces my lungs to move. The lack of control pushes panic through me once again as I lose control.

"She's stubborn," Garrett says as a door squeaks.

"This should help her," the female voice responds as the warmth takes over. "Next time she surfaces, I hope we can take out the ventilator tube."

This time the words make more sense, and my mind explodes with questions. Why am I on a ventilator? What happened? Where... The question dies before it forms as I crash under the silence.

My heavy eyelids refuse to move, but this time I'm ready to battle. The edge of panic sets in with each attempt to breathe, but I work against it. With a final effort, my eyelids blink open to a blurry room. There are three figures over on the right side, at the foot of my bed, speaking in hushed tones. I strain to hear them but can't make out the words. On the other side, two figures huddle together.

They all disappear as my eyelids fall shut in a long blink, and I struggle to open them again. When I do, I work to roll my head to the side. Beside me, a lone figure comes into view.

"Welcome back, Atlas. Don't struggle to breathe. Just let the machines work on you for a little longer."

Around us, all conversations stop. I roll my head back to look around the room, but my eyes close.

A soft kiss brushes against my forehead.

"Come on, beautiful. You've got this. It's time to return and fight," Reece says from beside me. His hand brushes through my hair, and I revel in his touch as I struggle to open my eyes.

When I win the battle once again, he's only inches from my face. Every detail is clear. I struggle to talk, but the tube prevents it. My hands clamp around it but are pulled off before I can get a good grip.

"I'll take it out soon," the female voice says. "I promise. Just let us run a few more tests, and we'll get it out so you can talk and breathe on your own."

I want to refuse, but the hands holding me down refuse to move. All I can do is give in to her request.

Time moves too slowly, and my body fights against the tube in my throat.

"I will have to sedate her," she says from beside me.

"She just woke up. We can't put her under again," Reece demands.

"It's the best course of action. It'll be a light sedation. Long enough to get the test results back but that's all," she says.

I try to shake my head to tell her I don't want to go back under, but it's already too late.

"I'll be right here, Atlas. I've got you," Reece says as I fade.

"Okay, Atlas. Let's get this thing out of you," the female says from beside me.

The air pump ceases, and she pulls on the tube. Pain screams across my throat as the tube rakes its way out. As soon as it clears my mouth, I attempt to take a breath. For the first couple attempts, I struggle to get my lungs full of air. An oxygen mask covers my face as I work through the searing pain until a breath finally fills my chest, and I relax into it.

"That's it. Breathe. Your throat will be sore for a while, and when you talk, you'll be hoarse. Those things will pass and won't be permanent."

I nod in response.

"You gave me quite a scare," Reece says as he squeezes my hand.

With an effort, I pull from his grasp and put my hands beside each other.

Garrett chuckles from the end of the bed, and I look up at him.

"I think she's trying to tell you that you are now even," he says as he looks at Reece.

I nod.

"Not funny, Atlas."

"Actually, for a woman who almost died, I think it's hilarious," Garrett replies.

"That's the point, asshole, she almost died," Reece growls.

"Gentlemen, let's not fight like children," Dominick says as he walks through the door. "Good to see you awake, Atlas. We should make a rule against you dying at the hands of a madman."

I glare at him, but he chuckles in response.

"Now that you're back with us, and some of us have had the appropriate forced nap," he says, looking over at Reece, "we've got a little business to attend to."

"This can wait, Dominick. She just woke up, and the ventilator hasn't been out of her mouth for five minutes," Reece spits.

"Welcome to the ruling class," Dominick replies without flinching. "I know speaking will come by the end of the day, but I want to give you a basic briefing now. We'll need you back in the Council chambers as quickly as possible."

He looks over at the woman beside me.

"How long before she's up and moving?" he asks.

"Twenty-four, maybe thirty-six hours. We'll start her on a protocol that will get her mostly on her feet."

"Good. Start now," he orders.

"Garrett, she'd requested a meeting with you and Kade after the last Council meeting. Set up some time with me on her calendar. We need to find out what she was thinking. I know it was something in that meeting."

I fold my arms across my chest and glare at Dominick.

"I'm sure I'll deserve the dressing down going through your head at this moment, Regent Major, and I will be glad to listen; however, right now, I am your voice."

With a huge effort, I fill my lungs and push out a sigh.

"Your irritation is noted," Dominick replies.

Unfolding my arms, I push the finger of my right into the palm of the other.

"Yes, my Regent, on the record."

I nod.

"Now, if you are quite done exercising power, we've got business to attend to. Someone is trying to get you out of the way, and based on reports from other areas, you aren't the only one in the crosshairs."

I pull my eyebrows together in a scowl.

"No, I don't like it any more than you do. It looks like you were the warning shot, but we're on the edge of a coup, and we've got to stop it before it gets started."

"You can't expect her to just jump back into this and solve every problem you throw at her," Reece says as he rises from his chair.

"I can, and I do. I know this is all new and very sudden, but there's nothing about these positions which are roses and paradise. Governing is hard, especially with the situations which are developing around us, but you two are the right people for the job. Your background in politics, thanks to your family and your sister, will be immensely helpful in our next maneuvers. Atlas' PR background, as well as her other previous work and connections, puts her in a good position to out think our opponents. We don't get down days or major days off. Every day for the rest of your life is a workday, even when we call it a vacation. So, either choose to stick around or walk now, Consort," Dominick shoots at Reece.

"Atlas?" Reece says as he picks up my hand.

My hand pulls from his and flies into various position as I scream at him through sign language.

"Don't Atlas me! You told me we were in this together! You said you understood. Welcome to our new life, Reece," Garrett says as he interprets my movements.

"Is that what she really said?" Reece asks without taking his eyes off of me.

"Well," Garrett starts, "there were a few more expletives in there, but I thought it best not to escalate the situation."

I point to Garrett without taking my eyes off of Reece.

"It was for your own good, my Regent," Garrett replies with a chuckle.

"Okay." Reece holds up both hands. "I'm used to giving people time to heal before jumping back in the saddle."

"She says we are out of time," Garrett translates.

"So it seems. Where you lead, I will follow, my Regent," Reece answers and plants a kiss on my forehead. "But we will discuss your recklessness when you are fully healed," he says with a whisper against my ear.

CHAPTER SIXTEEN

Three hours later, I sit dressed in a wheelchair. Around me, the PR apartment transforms from my makeshift hospital room back to my bedroom. The sitting room adjusts as adjustable laptop tables are added to each sitting position, along with one beside me. No one talks as people work around me. Every half hour, the nurse takes my vitals and checks on the IV hanging from the pole.

At the bar, Reece moves between animated in giving orders and sullen once they are in motion. The fear in his eyes when he stood over me haunts me, but there are bigger problems in front of me.

When the last worker exits the apartment, I take a deep breath from the oxygen mask. My limbs feel sluggish, but I am glad they respond to my mental commands. Now, if all the nerve endings would come off red alert, I'd be all set. It makes every touch painful, but I do not tell anyone in hopes it will subside as my other functions come back.

"Atlas?" Samantha screams as she bounds up the stairs and runs over to me. She engulfs me in a hug and pain sears through my body. With an effort, I only finch a little, but it's a relief when she lets go, only to have the pain race through my arms when she grabs them to look at me. "My God, woman, you know how to scare me to death! What is it with you and dramatic situations?"

"There's the pot calling the kettle black," I say in a hoarse whisper into the oxygen mask.

"You look like hell," she says.

"Thanks. Good to see you too," I say and try to force a smile.

When she lets go, I breathe a quiet sigh of relief and pull the mask from my face.

"What the hell happened?"

I shake my head in frustration. "I don't really know. One minute I'm walking down the hall, the next I wake up with a ventilator down my throat."

"Who did this to you?"

I shrug. "They say Edmund did it. Something about workers being paid off, a hidden bookcase door in the old apartment or something."

Samantha's face goes pale. "Edmund did this to you?"

"Yes, I guess. My memory is fuzzy, in more ways than one."

I hear footsteps ring out through the apartment and Samantha's eyes lift.

"You said you'd protect her," she growls.

"Yes, Samantha," Dominick says from behind me.

The click of a cane follows across the room.

"Samantha, it's not his fault," Reece says and places a firm hand on her shoulder. She flinches and drops her offensive posture.

"The hell it's not his fault, Reece. Ever since that asshole walked back into her life, it's been a disaster."

"Actually, Samantha, I went to him," I remind her.

"Atlas, what the hell is going on? Really? We used to be so close, but since all of this shit hit the proverbial fan, it's like we're in two different worlds."

I nod but don't comment.

"Please... talk to me," she pleads and slumps to the floor in front of me, her head on my lap.

The weight presses against nerves, but I suppress the cringe. She needs this, and I need to reassure her the best I can, even if I don't believe a word of it.

"I want to, Samantha. There's so much I want to tell you, but it's complicated."

"Then uncomplicate it for me," she says. The look in her eyes is full of pain and betrayal. We've been through so much together, and she knows I've left her behind in something.

I close my eyes and try to take a deep breath. When it falters, she pushes my hand with the oxygen mask to my face and I breathe.

Once again, I drop the mask to my lap and place my hand on Samantha's face.

"Give me a little more time. Everything in me wants you in my world always, close to me where you've always been and where I want you to always be, but I need time to sort out the complications."

"Let me help. Every skill I have is at your command. I don't know why Edmund is after you, but I'll do anything I can to help protect you. I need you, Atlas. You're my best friend and the way things are going, I'm scared I will lose you."

"Samantha," I say as I tuck my finger under her chin and force her to look up at me. "Our world is about to change. It will be harder than anything we've ever done, but I want you right there with me. To get there, you have to trust me."

I release her chin and wipe away the single tear sliding down her cheek.

"I trust you. It's why I followed you to DC, opened a business with you, and went gallivanting in your name. You've always held the world up. No matter what happens we always know you have it covered, but all of this is different. Something in you is changing."

"Indeed," I state and force a smile. "We all change, but I don't plan on dropping any more worlds. In fact, I'm trying to make them all stronger."

"If anyone can do it, you can," she says. "But if you die on me, I swear I'll piss on your grave every day while cussing you out."

I chuckle. "I'll make a note of it. You know life is terminal, right?"

"Fine. We'll renegotiate those terms in sixty or seventy years."

"Noted," I say and smile down at her. "Now I am loath to ask, but I need you to go back downstairs. There's a meeting I must attend."

"More secrets," she says with a sigh and moves to stand.

"We all wear masks, Samantha. You've always known the person behind them."

She nods. "Yeah. I'm realizing I don't enjoy being on the other side of it at all."

Reece chuckles. "Sucks, doesn't it?" he quips.

"Yeah," she says and bends down to kiss both cheeks. "Please let me in as soon as you can. I miss you."

"I miss you too... and I promise."

Samantha turns and heads down the stairs. When the door clicks closed, Garrett walks back up.

"Atlas," the nurse says as Garrett walks into the room. "On a scale of one to ten, what is your pain level?"

I wave my hand, as if the question annoys me. "Any pain I experience is manageable," I reply and turn my gaze to the seating area.

"Why the question, Asa?" Dominick addresses her by name without looking at me.

"Sir, she flinches any time something or someone touches her."

"Is that so?"

Asa nods, and I scowl at her observation.

"How long?" he asks.

"Since she woke up, but I chalked it up to the drugs in her system. While she may have some sluggishness and issues from the ventilator, most of the other drug side effects should have worn off. However, her reactions report otherwise."

"Answer the question, Atlas," Reece warns from the chair on my right.

"As I said, the pain levels are manageable."

Without warning, Dominick grabs my shoulder and squeezes.

Pain sears like a hot knife across my skin, and I scream. He lets go and I pant through the aftermath.

"Interesting management," he scoffs. "Asa, what do you think is the cause?"

"My area of expertise is lacking in nerve agents, but having said that, I believe you have the answer you feared."

Dominick nods as he takes a seat to my left.

"Say that again," Reece says and stares up at Asa.

"Consort, I believe he injected a nerve agent into the Regent. If my guess is right, I would say he did it after the knife cut. Even if she remembered the entire scenario, the amount of drugs swimming through her system would easily misinterpret events. I was hoping it would wear off with the other drugs, but her reactions tell me otherwise."

"What can we do?" he asks, concern and fear lacing each word.

"I'll contact my colleagues and give them the lab results, along with the current pathology. They are much better at this kind of situation."

"What is the worst-case scenario?" Dominick asks before Reece can form the question.

"If I am correct in my guess, her nerve endings are firing as if they are on alert most of the time. Any pressure, grab, change of position, etc., refires the nerve endings, even if they were worn out and starting to go dormant."

"Plain English," Reece demands.

"Sir, she cannot feel pleasure. Her body seems to currently process every touch as pain," Asa says.

"Every touch? Atlas?" he asks as he looks at me.

I take a deep breath and glare at all of them.

"If you all are done, we've got work to do. Asa, thank you, your information is noted," I say in a hoarse whisper and look up to show her my displeasure.

"Yes, my Regent," she replies with a bow and moves out of my view.

"Now," I say and pick up the papers from my laptop desk, "what is our first order of business, my counsel?"

"It looks like your health continues to be our first concern of order, my Regent," Dominick says and stares at me.

"Agenda item covered," I say with finality. "What is our second order of business?"

"We aren't done with the first one, Atlas," Reece argues.

"We are done because I say we are, my Consort. I suggest you read the information I presume you've been provided concerning protocol, etiquette and rules," I state. "Now if you all are done with your protective macho posturing, let's move on to what's actually important."

The door at the bottom of the stairs creaks open and then clicks closed. Everyone in the room goes silent as footfalls bound up the stairs. Seconds later, Kade enters the room as everyone stares at him.

"Please don't stop on my account," he says as he takes his place on the couch. "You summoned me, so here I am."

I smile over at him.

"And just in time too. We were moving the agenda on to item numbers two and three. As they are both bound, I'm not sure how to proceed," I say and look over at Dominick.

"First, we rock his world. Then we leave the mess on Garrett's doorstep," Dominick quips.

I nod in silent agreement and look over at Kade. "Kade, do you trust me?"

He raises an eyebrow. "That's a loaded question, Atlas."

I nod in agreement.

"You're not giving me any more than that? Seriously?"

Everyone takes my cue and sits in silence.

"Fine. Yes, I trust you."

"With your life?" I ask.

Kade scowls as he thinks about the question, then nods. "Yes, Atlas. With my life."

"Do you trust me with Jessica's life?"

"What does she have to do with anything?" he demands.

"Where the submissive goes, the Dominant must follow or be left behind, and the inverse is also true."

"But I'm not going anywhere. Am I?"

"Kade," I warn. We've played this game in the past. Anytime one of us was about to make life changing decision that would affect the other, the game of questions began until both of us agreed.

"How much will it change my world?"

"Irrevocably."

"For the better?"

"You know there's no way for me to put a judgment on a decision. It is foolishness to even ask," I reprimand.

Kade looks at the others in the room, but all of them refuse to meet his gaze. He looks back at me with a mixture of irritation and confusion.

"Yes, Atlas. I trust you."

"In all things?"

"You aren't my Dominant, but in all things outside that dynamic, I trust you above everyone else in my life."

"Will you help form my security team, Kade?"

"All that for a question which already has an answer? I'm already the head of your security, and the temporary club manager."

I shake my head and stare down at my hands for a long moment.

"Kade, you've always known everything about me. In the last few months, decisions were made which dramatically changed my world. I wasn't always privileged to them, and some were foisted upon me, but in the end I agreed. Now, for several reasons, I find I need to draw you into my new world."

"You aren't making any sense, Atlas," Kade replies.

"Her title, Kade, is Regent Major. She is equivalent to a monarch over the North American sector of the Sovereign Society. We believe in structured power-based relationships between those who choose to be in a contract and those who choose to buy such a contract," Garrett says in a matter-of-fact manner.

Kade stares at him for a long time and then laughs.

We all wait until he's done before anyone speaks.

"There's a reason I asked if you trusted me," I say.

"Atlas, this can't be serious. I mean, you got me. This is a great joke. We've talked about secret societies for the entire time I've known you. They were all either great fairy tales or good books to get us hot and bothered."

I watch Dominick raise an eyebrow out of the corner of my eye.

"It's all real. It is the reason Edmund is attacking me. The entire reason the club is filled with guests and secret meetings. It's not a conference, it's a high-level governing body who came here to install me into this ruling position, and I need your help to make me safe."

Kade watches me as I lay out the deepest secrets of my world.

"How long have you been a part of it?"

"The entire time I've known you. I didn't complete my membership, but it didn't seem to matter."

"You knew it was all real? Every joke? All of our late-night conversations?"

"Yes."

Kade rubs the bridge of his nose as he takes in the information. "Now that I know, what if I say no?"

"Then I'll be forced to break protocol and trust you will keep my secret," I reply.

Garrett and Dominick start to object, but I hold up a finger and stay their comments.

Kade watches their reactions and stares back at me as I lower my hand to my lap.

"You aren't kidding," he says as realization dawns.

"Not even a little bit, and I really need you in my corner."

I smile as relief washes over me.

"I made a vow, Atlas, and meant every word. I just never thought this would be the result."

"Neither did I, my dear friend, neither did I."

SILENCE STRANGLES THE ROOM AS EVERYONE AWAITS MY NEXT move.

"Garrett, I want you to know my request to Kade isn't a lack of trust in you, but I believe in the concept 'trust but verify.' Consider Kade my verification. No one should have had access to that apartment, nor known I would be in it. The only reason we were even there was because he compromised this apartment. A situation which I presume was since resolved?"

"Yes, Regent. The apartment was infested with surveillance bugs. We also interviewed anyone in your closer circle and checked their residences, as well as their workplaces. Dr. Hart's office was infested. She's beside herself at the privacy breeches, patient issues, and the fact she talked to Ian about your location in her office."

"I presume you ran a full background on Dr. Hart," I confirm without emotion.

"Yes, Ma'am. Because of the problem at her office, we ran a deep check. She's clean."

"And the rest of my friends, staff, and team?"

"Samantha is clean, but she's asking a thousand questions. Ian is noting every security request and fiscal investigation. Katie, your club assistant, has some anomalies in her background. Cassandra is following up on them. Melody turned in her resignation with the PR firm yesterday. This raised a red flag, and we've stepped up her investigation," Garrett reports.

"Wait. Melody quit?" I ask and look up from the report.

"Yes, Ma'am."

I shake my head and think of Samantha. She'll be like a caged animal soon if I can't get these worlds back in line.

"Dominick, find a Society member you trust to take over Melody's position. One who can keep their mouth shut."

"Of course, Regent," he says and makes a note.

"Anything else, Garrett?"

"Nothing of note. There's a bartender who was hired a couple months ago. Cassandra reported concerns during her operation in the club. We are running it to ground, but at the moment there's nothing there."

"Noted," I say and fidget. Each move sparks off new pains, and I wonder how I'll live the rest of my life unable to be touched again. There's no way Reece will stay if we don't find a solution, but there are bigger issues.

"Kade, you're up. Tell me what happened the night of the attack," I say as I push the errant thoughts away.

"You were stupid," he states.

Dominick's and Garrett's heads swing in his direction, but he doesn't remove his gaze from mine.

"I see you are irritated by my actions once again," I reply.

"You are foolish and reckless. If you are a monarch, or whatever, you'll be dead in under five years."

"Probably."

"Careful," Garrett growls.

"Truth to power." Kade smirks.

"I see you are in the mood to ride the line of respect," I level at him. "With more respect this time, tell me what I did wrong."

"For someone who's trained in going to ground and personal security at your level, Atlas, you were dumb. This entire time you've done one thing after another to put yourself in the worst position. The problem lies in the fact that all the experts I know aren't surprised. They tell me the more you know about the field the more likely you are to be overly paranoid or stop thinking when it becomes personal."

"Fair," I comment but don't elaborate.

"I put Tanner in the position outside the door, so he would walk you back to the apartment and be the first one through the door. Second, you left Reece down the hall. His current pace can't match yours based on his injury. Though now I'm sure he's faster than a wheelchair since he can get down the stairs."

I glare at him. "You aren't amusing."

"Yes I am," he replies and flashes me a grin. "Look. I know you are comfortable in the club and you've paid big money to equip it with the latest technology. That area of the club wasn't upgraded because we wanted one area off the grid, in case someone hacked us. Which we were, in a couple different places and before you ask, we're already on it."

"Then what happened? Since no one here has commented that Edmund was found, I am presuming he is still at large. There's only one door in and one door out of that apartment. Either he disappeared into thin air or you all need to get a better fitness program," I return the lob in Kade's word game.

Kade clenches his jaw and mimics the same with each fist.

"He disappeared into thin air. At least, until an hour ago, it was our only working theory."

"Don't make me pull teeth, boy," I comment, and his head jerks up to meet my gaze.

"We discovered a door behind the dresser an hour ago. It appears, during the recent renovations, someone gave the room a 'backdoor.' It goes into a storage closet on the other side of the wall. We keep our uniforms in that closet, and we're missing two full sets."

"Well, that solves the mystery of the disappearing madman. The next question is how did he know I'd come through the door first?"

Kade shakes his head. "I don't think he knew. The working theory is that Edmund believed Reece would enter first, and you'd follow. He carried a knife because it is a quiet weapon."

"Okay. How was I drugged? The knife blade?"

"We thought that was true at first," Garrett replies. "But found the water in the pitcher on the counter was full of various drugs. Our only conclusion is that you drank a glass of water and became easier prey."

I scoff. "Willingly drink a glass of water when a madman is threatening me? I don't think so."

"Do you remember anything from the attack?" Dominick asks.

"No." I shake my head and stare down at the oxygen mask in my

141

lap. "Everything is an odd blur. Flashes of a word or sound. Each time I focus on something, I lose more of it."

My hand rubs the bandages across my chest to settle an itch. The pressure fires a searing line across the cut, and I gasp for breath.

"Manageable," Dominick mumbles.

"How bad is it?" I ask without looking up.

"We've done everything we can to this point to make sure it doesn't leave a scar, but it's a deep wound."

"Scars are sexy I guess," I say in an attempt to find the silver lining.

"It's his initial, Atlas," Kade says.

Everyone refuses to meet my gaze. I shake my head in utter disbelief.

"No. No!"

I stare at Reece as a tear spills down my face.

"It'll be okay," Reece says in frustration.

"He wasn't joking. We are really playing a game of thermonuclear war." I strangle on the words.

Guilt, pain, and devastation crash through me until I find the thread to morph it into anger.

"He's not doing this alone. If he is, then you are incompetent, Kade and Garrett, and you should resign immediately from the Obsidian Overwatch. If he's not, then you all need to find who is behind these attacks, so I can take off their heads."

CHAPTER SEVENTEEN

Four hours later, exhausted, I dismiss everyone from the apartment.

"You need to meet with the Council tomorrow," Dominick advises as he walks past.

"I know," I acknowledge with a nod. "Why is this happening to me?"

"Because you were the weakest link."

"Please, don't hold back on how you really feel about me," I chide.

"My Regent, you misunderstand. The Society decided without you. We all thought it in your best interest. To give you more time and experience in the outside world. Everything around us is changing at a rapid pace. We are lucky to hold to the ancient ways this long, but the encroachment is happening. Some of us thought it would be best to bring in someone who understands success in the soft world. Who might even be able to help us find those who look for something deeper and bring them willingly into our world. We can't be afraid of change and survive. Not anymore. The light is coming to the shadows," he says.

"Why me?"

"We all believe you the most equipped. You were strong enough to walk away from us, even when your soul demanded we were the right path. There's nothing you won't attempt, study, research, or run to the deepest detail until it satisfies you. Your strength comes from your dominance on the surface and equally from what you find from your knees. Like an iceberg, most are periodically privileged to see above the waterline, but it is the fierceness below it for which one should watch."

"Yet, my counsel, you call me your weakest link while flattering me in lines about strength."

"We are the reason for your weakness, my Regent. Our failure to protect you, to bring you into your rightful position when the decision was originally made and provide an Obsidian guard team. But we plead for your forgiveness in our folly. It was your best interest we bore in mind."

"So you lost a madman. He found me because the Sovereign Society made me a Regent Major unbeknownst to me. Then I am attacked under false provocation. When I turn to you for help, you issue an ordeal for my weakness? Am I always to pay for the sins of others?"

"Atlas, stop. Think. You came to me desperate and afraid. Offered me no details, and your friends were frantic in their search for you. At the point you arrived, you'd been off the grid for weeks. An unbalanced mess. We both know you need both sides of you balanced to be at your best. You use each for perfect perspectives in our world," Dominick says, his tone tinged with regret.

"Thank you for the insight, my counsel. You are dismissed," I say without looking up at him.

Dominick pauses for a long moment, then bows and backs towards the stairs. At the last moment, he pivots, and I hear his footfalls echo in the stairwell. When the click of the door echoes through the apartment, I let out the breath I'm holding.

"My Regent, I can give you something for the pain, but it will most like create a sedative effect," Asa says as she walks in front of me.

I shake my head. "Not right now. There's work to do," I say and pick up my tablet.

"I must insist," she starts, and I put up my hand, staying her objection.

"Please leave us."

Asa looks over at Reece, who shakes his head. Then she returns to look at me, gives a slight bow, and follows in the wake of Dominick's departure.

"She's right. You need to rest," Reece says from his chair.

"I've slept for several days, based on these reports. I was Regent all of one day and the world went to hell. Then my counselor tells me I'm their weakest link. On top of that, there's an 'E' carved into my skin, not to mention the... well, an unnerving situation, so to speak," I huff and bite my lip to hold back the tears which threaten to spill.

"I'm sorry I couldn't protect you," Reece whispers.

"You protect me in all the ways which matter," I say and force a smile.

"If my leg wasn't--" he starts.

"Carved up like my breast by a madman?" I finish. "Going through the door first probably saved a life. The cost to me was minimal in comparison."

Reece looks up. Confusion is written across his face. "Why do you say such a thing?"

"Edmund, and whoever else is behind this, doesn't want me dead. Everyone else would be collateral damage. As long as I'm the one in the line of fire, I'll only come out with pain and suffering, but I won't be dead."

He shakes his head. "You didn't see what I saw when I walked through the door, Atlas. You can't be sure he doesn't want you dead."

"What did you see, Reece? No one will tell me what happened."

Beside me he grows quiet. Everything in me wants to run to him and curl up in his lap. I want his arms around me while he tells me it

is all a bad dream. Edmund took away my most basic need in life...
touch and closeness. Being held in a way I never knew growing up.

"There was blood... all over you. I was sure he'd sliced your neck,"
he says, taking a deep breath. "It soaked your blouse as it bound your
arms behind you. When we first arrived, we thought you were dead.
It took everything Kade's team had to break down the door. Edmund
disabled the electronic keypad with a magnetic device of some sort."

Flashes of the boat crowd my mind. Blood runs in rivers across
the deck. People scream at me to let him go. The crew is below decks.
With each passing moment of his description, the scenes take on
more vividness. A medic screams, "You've got to let him go, Ma'am."

Panic swarms my brain, and I fight for my next breath. Pain sears
down my throat. A hand forces a mask to my face as I try to force the
images away.

"Breathe, Atlas. We will get through this. Stay with me, beautiful," Reece's voice coaches next to my ear. "I'm right here. You are safe
and so am I. I'm sorry for what I must do."

Pain screams through my arm. Seconds later my world fades to
black.

"COUNCIL, THANK YOU FOR ASSEMBLING," I SAY AS I WALK INTO
the room two days later. "I apologize for the lateness of our reconven-
tion, but I was... detained."

Chairs push back from the table at the sound of my voice, and all
conversations cease. Each member stands and snaps to attention as I
make my way to the front of the room with every ounce of focus I
possess. My legs ache from a lack of movement, and my skin is a
searing fire, but I make sure the expression on my face remains
neutral. The black turtleneck and matching dress pants present an
imposing figure along with Alexandra's style. On my left shoulder sits
the pin of the Regent Major.

I step to the head of the table and look down the line. No one dares to look back at me.

"My counsel, I believe you were on the second item on the agenda," I say without taking my seat.

"Yes, my Regent," Dominick replies.

"Then proceed."

He breaks his position and looks over at me. I return it with an emotionless stare and raise a single eyebrow.

"As you wish, my Regent," he says and returns to attention. "Security details from across the world report major and minor attacks on various Regent Majors. The provocations are unknown at this time, but investigations are in full process."

"How many perpetrators are in custody?" I interrupt.

"Two, Ma'am."

"Are they Society members?"

"They are," Dominick confirms.

"Which Houses trained them?"

Several members break their stance and look down the table until they meet my hard gaze, then snap back to attention.

"The House of Roses trained two persons currently in custody," Dominick says.

"If memory serves, when a member of the house is brought before the Tribunal, doesn't the Head of the Household also stand on trial for a decision on their worthiness to continue the House line?"

"Yes, Regent."

"What house trained Edmund?"

"No one has given you this information, Regent."

"Good, then you can give it to me now," I say and stare down the table.

Around me, there is no movement. Not a single body shifts, but the tension becomes palpable. The answer to this question will bring to bear my suspicions. I was still fuming at the lost time from Reece's sedation stunt, but I'd pored over the history of several houses the previous day. Putting off the Council was a good move, if my hunch was right.

"He was trained under the House of the Rising Star," Dominick replies.

An audible sigh ripples around the room.

"They are second in the succession of the global Regent position, much like the House of Roses is to mine, if memory serves," I state.

"Yes, Ma'am," Dominick says, and I watch a scowl crease his brow.

"Then I know both Houses honor and serve. These must be unhappy coincidences of circumstance," I say and nod. "Especially as both heads of those houses stand in my Court, and I am sure their fealty pledge to me would be honorable and true."

"With due respect, Regent, this is not a medieval court," a woman says from mid-table.

"True," I answer, "but in the investiture ceremony, each Head of Household states such. How does it go? 'I promise in pledge to my member seal, I will be faithful to my Regent. I will never cause them harm and will observe my homage to them in completion, good in faith and without deceit.' May I remind you all, this oath stood the moment I accepted and ascended into this position. We are not in medieval times, as your peer so eloquently pointed out, but my power is not diminished because this Council exists. The thing about living in the shadows is when something happens, it does so in the cover of darkness."

"Is that a threat, Regent?" Walter Jackson asks.

"No. It's a promise. Ask anyone in this establishment; they will tell you I am fiercely loyal and protective. Many situations may have me on the back foot, but such a problem doesn't last forever," I reply without looking at him.

Dominick clears his throat, and a smile tugs on one side of my lips.

"How rude of me for interrupting your session, as I do preside over it. Please continue," I say without sitting.

Next to me, he breaks attention once again and looks over at me. The question is as clear as if he'd said it out loud, and I smile. If I am going to suffer in pain for revenge or some version of odd entitlement at the hands of someone in this room, then they can all suffer under the beauty of protocols.

FOR THE NEXT TWO HOURS I ENDURE THE ENDLESS DISCUSSIONS of governmental grievances, policies, and the current security threats across the organization. Pain is a constant companion by the time we've reached the end of the agenda. My legs are burning from my refusal to sit, and every nerve is in concert with the ache of my muscles. It takes every effort I hold not to grimace or give in to the chair which touches the back of my knees.

I force a dispassionate mask as stoic as I've ever given to anyone as I breathe through each spasm. There's no way I can live the rest of my life in such a place, though the reality of the possibility must be addressed soon. This is the position I've accepted, and it won't get easier from here.

"Are there any further discussions?" Dominick says from beside me.

Silence lingers in the room, periodically punctuated by a restless movement or the slide of a chair across the floor.

"My Regent, the Council bids a dismissal by your hand," he says to me without looking over.

I nod.

"I thank you for your time and service. You are dismissed," I say and shift my body. Pain engulfs me as every nerve ending lights. I stifle the scream which wants to rip from my throat and force my legs to obey my internal commands. With the last ounce of effort, I step around my chair and away from the table.

Immediately every member of the Council bows their head and moves around their chairs. No one lingers or holds a conversation. Beside me, Dominick doesn't move. When the last Council member walks out the door, I grab the back of the chair and pant through the pain. My eyes close and allow me to focus inward to find some level of control.

"My counsel, please tell the two houses mentioned at the top of this meeting that I would like a private audience," I command through clenched teeth.

"My Regent, I advise against this action at the moment," he replies, concern lacing his tone.

"Dominick, I have heard you. Now obey."

I know he's glaring at me without looking at him. Everything in him battles against this side of me, but I can't show weakness here, not now. It doesn't matter what I'm going through; I serve the Society, and those closest to me need to understand the depths of the commitment.

"Shall I call for a wheelchair?" Dominick asks.

"No. I'll walk."

"You can barely stand."

"I refuse to show weakness. This is not an exceptional situation," I say as I make small steps toward the door.

"Atlas, your stubbornness will cause you more harm than good."

"Your concern is noted."

"Stop it! You're being reckless and stupid. There's no sense putting yourself through this when you are surrounded by those who can protect you," Dominick says. His voice echoes off the walls.

I pivot and nearly lose my balance as I grab the back of the closest chair.

"Protect me? Protect me! I get my actions were stupid when I thought this whole situation was a deranged stalker, but look around, Dominick. My world, in a matter of months, has been flipped on its head. They have thrust me back into a world I walked away from, and now it's under attack. Nothing and no one can protect me. Either you stand with me and help me catch up on everything I need to know to adequately play this game, or you leave me alone. Right now I'm trying to reconcile that the one person I love, the person whose life I've stolen for this nonsense, may never be able to touch me again.

Which leaves me exactly one option, and it is not only the right one, but the only fair one."

"He won't go," Dominick replies.

"Let me be clear. He won't have a choice. The only reason he's caught up in the mess is me, and if I'm barely a person, there's no way I will make him stay. Now, please do my bidding. I will be ready for a private audience in two hours. Am I clear, my counsel?"

"Crystal clear, but don't think this is the end of it," he threatens.

"Watch your tone. You're on my turf here, and I know exactly how much power I hold."

"One should remember power and control are an illusion," he says as he bows.

"Exactly, and I hold illusions incredibly well," I reply and turn to walk out the door with every ounce of grace I can muster.

"Ask," Reece says as my foot finally hits the top step of the apartment staircase.

"Excuse me?"

"You heard me, Atlas. This is the Consort's chamber. Request permission to enter it," he replies as he watches me from his seat on the couch.

"I am tired, Reece. Can we play these games later?" I reply and take a step forward.

"Stop."

My entire body freezes at the command, and I berate the shift as I battle to be back on top. I grab the wall to steady myself.

"Reece," I say, trying to force a non-existent calm into my voice, "can we discuss this later? I'm expecting a private audience with two household heads, and the Council meeting was long."

"All you need to do is ask."

"But this is my only private space," I challenge.

"Yes, by design. It is the one place where your power is exchanged for mine. Where you know you are safe in more than one way," he says.

My hand reaches up and rubs against the large bandage under my shirt. Fear threatens to overwhelm me, but I push it back. Everything in me wants to protect him, but the failure of my last attempts lingers between us.

"My Consort, permission to enter your suite?"

Reece watches me. The weight of his gaze is like being stripped one layer at a time with no ability or desire to stop it.

"Permission granted. From this moment forward, this is how you will always enter this space. Let it be a reminder that to the outside world you may be fierce, and within this space I may allow the same, but I am the one who controls all within it. Do you agree?"

There is something about the interaction which sets me at ease, even as part of me rails against it.

"I agree."

"Good, then please join me," he says and motions to the sitting area.

With reluctance, I let go of the wall and walk to the sitting area.

"Asa, please provide as much relief to Atlas as you can without sedating her," he says but doesn't take his eyes off of me.

I shake my head at the thought of another needle penetrating my skin.

"No," I whisper. "Please. I'm fine."

Reece quirks an eyebrow at my reply.

"There's no choice for you in this matter," he says as Asa prepares my arm.

Seconds later, the sharp stab of pain is quickly followed by relief as the nerves go from sharp pricks to a dull body ache. I close my eyes and lean back against the chair.

"Better?" Reece asks, and I nod my response.

"Asa, please get the Regent food and water. I am sure her lack of self-care extends far past this episode of pain management."

"Yes, Consort," she says from beside me, and her footsteps thud softly across the floor.

My body relaxes in the change of state.

"We're not doing this again, Atlas," he says without preamble. "So let me be clear, I'm not going anywhere. This might not be the path I would have chosen, but we're in it together."

"Why?" I ask as I open my eyes and look at him.

"Because I want to be here. I desire to stand by you and watch you in every facet of your complex personality."

"And if I can never tolerate your touch for any length of time? How long will it last before you will tell me I'm cold and frigid or it becomes too much work?"

"Then it would be a problem I created out of my own weakness. If I can't bring you in the direction, I want you without a touch, then I'm doing it wrong. Don't get me wrong, Atlas, I want to bring you every imaginable physical, emotional, and mental pain and pleasure at my hand, but we all have our limits. We will adjust."

"I can't see that path from here," I say, holding back tears as my heart aches over the loss I envision.

"You can't imagine an anal hook in your ass tied to a ring in the back of your chair while you hold an audience with someone or even under a formal gown? How can you not imagine me grabbing your hair and bending you over a counter while shoving a butt plug in your ass, while assuring you I will increase it to the next size every hour on the hour? All the while making you defend your position on the latest problem. I find it difficult to believe you can't imagine that I will tell you to strip at the door and masturbate after you controlled your entire court or dressed one of them down. There are so many possibilities ahead of us," he says.

"If you can't touch me, they do not exist," I say as the images assault me and press on my head space.

"Girl, don't lie to me or yourself." His tone shifts, and with it, so do I.

"Yes, Sir," I reply, and my eyes fall before looking back up at him.

"Ah, that's much better. We will get through this, Atlas."

CHAPTER EIGHTEEN

I shake my head to hold back tears which threaten to stream down my face.

"You'll grow tired of me," I whisper and close my eyes against the roller coaster of emotions.

"Kneel!" Reece commands.

My eyes fly open, and I stare at him. The prospect of the weight on my knees makes me brace for the pain.

"You can't be..."

"Did I stutter, Atlas? Do I ever say what I do not mean?" he asks as he points to the floor in front of him.

With reluctance, I push out of my chair and stand. Nerve endings flair as the signal fights against the pain medication working through my body.

"Please," I whisper.

"Now, Atlas."

I nod and work my body down. Each bend or brush against furniture lights new pain. When my knees hit the floor and my body settles over them, I cry out as searing agony wracks through me.

Reece watches from the couch with dispassionate interest. He taps on a tablet in his lap and then returns to observe me. The tears I held back earlier spill over and release in streams down my face.

"A proper kneel. Shoulders back. Sit back on your heels. You know this position. I expect perfection," Reece says.

"I can't. It's too much. Please," I beg.

"Things you will remember in the future when you wonder if I am capable of my job."

I barely hear the footstep behind me over my own sobs and focus on the throbbing pin pricks as I bite back screams.

"What the hell is going on here?" Dominick says from behind me. "Let her up right now!"

"These are my chambers, counselor. You'd be wise to remember your place," Reece warns without taking his eyes off of me.

"Reece," Dominick starts, and Reece raises an eyebrow. "Consort, I beg for mercy on her behalf."

"Your plea is noted but denied. She's stubborn, scared, and lost. In addition, there is a belief I cannot put the parameters in place to deal with both rewards and punishments. That my love for her will somehow make me weaker and incapable of exerting the necessary measures. Right now, she's realizing I am willing and capable of using her body's issues against her. It a àpropos punishment, as she felt she could use the same to bring the Council in line, if your report is honest."

Behind me, Dominick sighs and sits in the chair at the edge of my peripheral view.

"Please. I... can't..." I sob.

"Consort, for your awareness, the Regent has a meeting in an hour with the head of two houses."

"Push the meeting off until tomorrow morning," Reece says, his gaze unwavering.

"You have... no... you... can't," I grind out and scream as his foot taps the top of my thigh.

"My domain," he reminds me and looks up at Dominick. "I presume the meeting was to be held here."

"Yes, Consort," Dominick confirms.

"Then, in the future, you will check with me or anyone who handles my schedule for use of private space to do Society business. You'll find me easier to deal with if you will ensure my role is clearly understood by all involved, and I am briefed on larger issues which will affect the Regent. I do not come from this world, and if my methods rake against your sensibility, rules, or protocols, then you should have thought it through before dragging us into it."

He removes his foot, and I pant through the searing agony.

"You're a cruel bastard," Dominick remarks.

"Not cruel. Often underestimated--and therein lies the difference. Atlas was under the false belief that I would leave because of her affliction. She sought to challenge my rule, by agreement, in my space just as she demanded the same authority of the Council. If she can put herself through pain for power, then she can endure it in reverse. Such is not cruel; it is a lesson in my understanding of the nuances of all of her. If I let it go, and she continues to believe things which are untrue, the resulting distress would be cruel. This situation is a creative discipline by teaching a lesson she will not soon forget."

His words cut as deep as the physical pain. He is not wrong. I did underestimate his commitment and fortitude. Moreover, I assumed I could challenge him and win.

"Rise and return to your seat, Atlas," Reece says with a nod.

"Yes... Sir," I reply with a gasp.

"Brutality, when used with compassion, love, and understanding, is often the best thing for a relationship. None of us are new to the necessities of power exchange relationships. Our current collective situation doesn't allow for lessons to be repeated in a softer manner. Besides, no one knows if there's a cure for Atlas' condition. It is best she accepts and realizes I can do my job. It is because I love her so deeply that I must do whatever is necessary, even when the result looks like brutality from outward appearances," Reece says to Dominick, but he watches me. "Isn't that right, Atlas?"

Every nerve ending in my body screams. Tears spill in rivers down my face. The stoic power and control I displayed earlier now sits in utter devastation. I am stunned. Never in my life have I been seen to the depth Reece has demonstrated.

Dominick always pushed me to the brink but gave at the last second. At the time I thought it was because I couldn't handle it, but after, I realized that dynamic relationships struggle when love is introduced. It made the whole thing feel incomplete. Growth ceased for softness and romance. Neither partner demanded anything more of the other because they wanted to accommodate. Then dissatisfaction set in and the whole thing fell apart. I didn't know there was another way.

As I sit sobbing until there are no tears left, I know Reece is right. His ability to compassionately use my affliction against me shows he cares on an incomprehensible level. It wasn't done with malice but a true understanding of what I needed. Without a doubt, I realize he is willing to do whatever it takes to protect me against the world. More important than that is his willingness to protect me from myself and ensure I can lean on our relationship in every way when the world is hard.

I nod in response, and Reece quirks an eyebrow.

"Yes, Sir. Thank you... for everything," I acknowledge as the joy in my heart fights the pain in my body.

"I will always hold you to a higher standard because you would accept no less from yourself or me. Every action or decision has a consequence; my job is to make sure you remain balanced, on whatever side is necessary, through them," Reece says and offers a soft smile.

"Thank you," I say as my voice catches on a hiccup.

Reece leans forward and hands me a white linen handkerchief. I take it with regret as I wipe my eyes, and my mascara ruins the cloth.

"That's why we use bleach," he says when I scowl. "Now, counselor, I believe you came here for a purpose, which was not to watch the Regent suffer. Care to share it?"

I turn to Dominick, who sits with his fingers steepled in front of his face and watches me.

"I didn't take our Regent for a masochist, based on personal knowledge," Dominick says.

"She's not. At least not in the traditional sense. There's nothing in what you witness that gave Atlas any relief or pleasure, outside the fact I made her certain I will not let her fall. In her mind, she was already watching me walk out the door because I love her, but as you know, she needs to take internal emotions and transform them. When they are made physical, there is a release. To let the things go unnoticed, to be inconsistent, to allow a pass on behavior, and such, is paramount to telling her she means nothing to me. If I were to guess, the minute someone declared their love to her in the past is the first minute they stopped giving her what she needed."

The racing thoughts in my mind skip a beat and tumble one upon another. I'd voiced nothing to Reece, and yet he read my soul like words in a book. Being stripped naked in a crowd would be less vulnerable than how I feel at this moment.

"Is this true, my Regent?" Dominick looks with a dispassionate gaze between the two of us.

"Indeed," I whisper, barely able to force the acknowledgment through my lips.

"I see," he replies and pulls out his phone. A few taps on the screen later, he looks up. "The head of the House of Roses and the House of the Rising Star will meet with you tomorrow. Is there a particular location which best suits?"

"She'll meet them in her office in the club," Reece answers.

"As you wish, Consort," he replies and taps on the screen. "Now that I've settled the meeting, I've received a package from the medical team Asa sent your information to."

"Asa," Reece says, "will you please join us? We will most likely need your medical expertise to understand what is in the file."

Footfalls echo off the walls as Asa approaches. She places a portable tray with a glass of water and a plate of celery with peanut butter beside my chair.

"I can give the Regent another dose to help manage the pain," she says to Reece.

He shakes his head.

"No. It is best that she push through it on her own."

"As you wish, Consort," she replies with a slight bow of her head and takes a seat at the other end of the couch when Reece motions to it.

When Asa is settled, Dominick hands the large manila envelope to her. She pulls out a stack of papers and reads the medical report.

Reece turns and points to the tray beside me. I know better than to argue and pick up the glass of water. It is cool on my tongue. I take it in large gulps until the glass is empty.

When I look up, I face a frown from Reece. My actions confirm everything, and I know there will be a consequence at some point.

"I see we need to revisit the necessity of rules," he says and turns back toward Asa.

Periodically, she makes small sounds as she reads over the report. Some are positive; others concern me. I want to scream for the truth, but I wait with as much grace as I can muster as I fight my body.

"This report is a little concerning. According to my colleagues, the Regent is experiencing significant microglial activation. Her nerves appear to be acting in a damaged capacity and sending out ATP and fractalkine, resulting in inflammation, which is what is causing the pain sensations. Based on the blood work and history we sent over, no one believes there is any nerve damage. However, her body is reacting in the same way chronic pain patients do, and they fear that if we can't stop it, then it will set up a response loop and actual nerve damage will occur," Asa says without looking up from the papers.

"In layman's terms, if you please, Asa," Reece says, his tone gentle but firm.

"My apologies, Consort. Something is causing her nerves to over excite, which is transmitted as pain. Whatever is happening mimics the same things chronic pain patients experience after an injury. The nerve cells signal an issue, and her body's response is to create inflammation which exacerbates the problem. The recommendation is to start her on an anti-inflammatory regimen immediately and back it with pain management. In addition, a change in diet to also help reduce the inflammation. They also suggest a significant reduction in stress."

Everything in me releases in uncontrolled laughter. All three heads swivel towards me, but there's nothing I can do to make it stop, no matter how much pain it causes. Around me, no one moves. I fight to control the eruption, but each time I think about the comment on stress, I fall into a fit of laughter all over again.

"She's hysterical," Dominick says in a dry drawl.

Reece shakes his head. "Quite the opposite. She's finally coming to terms with it all. I almost feel sorry for whoever she faces tomorrow."

Sunlight pours across my face, and I blink against the onslaught. For the first time since this whole ordeal started, the thoughts running through my mind are calm. There's a sense of peace. Reece's brutal demonstration pushed me to the very edge and dangled me above the abyss but never dropped me. After Asa's report, we discussed options over dinner. When I tried to push further, Reece ended my protests with a command to sleep, reinforced by a needle full of sedatives.

I stretch and bite back a groan at the racing pin pricks which greet me.

"Good morning, beautiful. How did you sleep?" Reece asks from the chair in the corner of the room.

"I slept well, thank you," I reply. "Not that I had much choice."

Reece looks up from his tablet and grins. "A good Dominant uses all the tools at their disposal to ensure proper results are obtained."

"At any cost?" I shoot back.

"Not at the cost of harm to their submissive," he replies and steeples his fingers in front of his mouth.

I sit up and pull the sheet around me. There's a change in Reece. Once, where there was a cool exterior, now there's an almost predatory demeanor.

"Have you told your family about all this?" I ask in an attempt to take his focus away from me.

"A version. They were not thrilled with my decisions but support me," he replies.

I nod. He follows each movement, and I am aware of the weight of his gaze.

"This morning, you will attend to your morning routine. Your outfit for the day is in the bathroom on the back of the door. When you are ready, we will have a brief breakfast and then walk over to your office in the club together. As is my right to hold audience with you, according to the information provided to me, I will do so when you meet with the head of the households," he says, and I try to object.

Reece holds up a finger and scowls. "I fully believe you can handle this, and much more complex situations yourself, but I would like to be another pair of eyes. Ones which can watch the body language and listen to the words without a need to focus on the next move," he says as he stands.

"I am at your service, my Regent," Reece says and bows slightly at the waist. "Now get dressed, pet. We've got dragons to slay."

A smile spreads across my lips as I watch him walk out the door. With a flourish, I throw off the covers. Immediately my body reminds me that I must adjust to its new problems, but I refuse to let it dampen the joy his words and action shoot through me.

For the next hour, I shower and get dressed. I focus on the easy transformation from Atlas to Alexandra, even though the circle of people who look at them interchangeably is growing. Every member of the club must be protected from what is happening right under their noses, and it is for them that I am painstaking in my efforts.

I pull on the black wool pants suit which is paired with a dark red blouse and black stiletto heels. For a long moment, I stare at the shoes. Where once they brought a sense of power as I towered over my opponents, now they are torture which must be managed to prove my strength.

With a deep breath, I slip on the shoes and walk across the bedroom. Reece turns toward me as I step into the main part of the apartment.

"Stunning," he says and motions to a stool at the bar.

I paste on a smile and fight the inevitable agony.

"Asa, please prepare the medication for the Regent's day according to her schedule," Reece says as he sets a plate of food in front of me. "She's got people to pull into line, and we need to give her all the help we can."

"At once, Consort."

CHAPTER NINETEEN

"Your appointment is here, Ma'am," Katie says from the door of my club office.

"Please show them in," I reply without looking up from the paper in front of me.

"Yes, Ma'am," she says and motions to the people waiting in the hallway. "She will see you now."

I rise from my seat and look toward the door.

Walter Jackson, the head of the House of Roses, and Kimberly Michaels, the head of the House of the Rising Star, both walk through the door one after another. They each stop at my desk, and I hold out my hand as they kiss the back of it. With an effort, I breathe though my body's reaction and work not to cringe.

"Thank you for coming, ladies and gentlemen," I say and sit down at my desk. Both of them continue to stand before me, awaiting a command which is not forthcoming.

"We are at your service, Regent," they say in near unison as they bow slightly from the waist.

"Dispense with the crap. Neither of you, based on the information I've received, is at my service," I say, and both heads jerk up. Their glares tell me everything I want to know. "If my intelligence is to be believed, each of you have a vested interest in actively working against me and the Regent Global. In addition, Mr. Michaels, you'll soon be up on charges for the fault of your house in the recent assault of a former member of your house in my recent attacks. While you, Mr. Jackson, your house would gain a Regent Major position for the first time in more than a hundred and fifty years if I step down from the Regency."

"All of these things are true by our association of the situations which play out around us, but we can only be held accountable to the code of association and nothing more," Walter Jackson replies as he shifts his weight between his legs. "None of this information is secret or scandalous, unlike what the Regent herself, along with her current Consort, have endured in the last few months."

"And yet, here I am. Called back to the Sovereign Society after I walked away, when they demanded my service as Regent."

"If you didn't have your little power-hungry guard dog, Dominick Dawes, on the Council, you would have been left to rot in the soft world where you belong," he spits. "Maybe you should take the attack as a warning and return to it."

I lean back in my chair and look up at the men who stand before me. One is full of insults and the other stands in a rest position with his eyes front. On the surface they are the epitome of absolute adoration and perfect manners.

"What say you, Mr. Michaels? Do you believe me to be unfit?"

"Regent, you were chosen by most of the Council, and I abide by our collective decision. Please accept the deepest, most sincere, apology on behalf of my House for the recent attack from our former member," Kimberly Michaels replies.

"Why did Edmund attack me?" I ask without aiming the question.

"Maybe he was brave enough to do what the rest of us won't," Walter Jackson says with an air of arrogance.

Kimberly shakes his head.

"Edmund, or as we knew him, Carl, was always an eccentric

member of our house. An owner within my line purchased his contract because he was great with numbers. He had a head for business and planning, which was good for business. However, it was discovered in the second year of the contract that he craved darker interactions. When his contract owner was unwilling to meet his needs... well, you know the results, my Regent."

I nod.

"My house has paid for its original crimes. The member was surrendered to the Tribunal of the Society and removed. I do not see how we can continuously be held accountable for a situation over which we have no control," Mr. Michaels says as his gaze lands on me.

There's something cold and calculating in his eyes which rubs against his outside charming demeanor. It is the same look I remember from Edmund when I refused his original proposal, and it sends a shiver through me.

"When is the last time you had contact with Edmund?" I ask, forcing the uneasiness down.

"The Tribunal refused to grant us contact rights based on their assessment of our inability to know the mental state of our members. While we argued such was an impossibility, Dominick Dawes, the tribunal head judge, condemned my line for ten years. We can have no contact with Edmund and no Dominant in my house can purchase a new contract without a full evaluation from two different full panels of doctors, both physically and mentally focused, at their expense. In addition, all re-terms of current contracts are at the discretion of the Regent Major of their area. When you are fully invested, I am sure you will find several requests from my house awaiting you," he replies. His delivery is cordial and factual, but there's something which unsettles me.

"It is my understanding from the tribunal notes, that Edmund's behavior was horrid," I say with a calmness I don't feel.

"There's some dispute about the accuracy of the account,"

Kimberly responds. "Edmund denied the charges and said the photos were digitally altered."

"Why?"

"That's a question for the Obsidian Overwatch. They ran the investigation. There were a number of inconsistencies with their findings."

"As with any investigation, I'm sure," I reply. "What I don't understand is why he's targeting me now? I had nothing to do with the investigation or the tribunal decision. In fact, I'd left the Society and entered the soft world again."

"Maybe he thought revenge was a good course or that your removal would ensure a change," Walter sneers.

I shake my head. "That makes no sense. Why would I be his target? I gave him everything he ever asked for in session, right up until he asked to marry me."

"I can imagine being removed from the Society he loved by Mr. Dawes, then being rejected by his perfect prodigy was more than anyone could handle," Kimberly comments.

"I'm not Mr. Dawes' prodigy. Quite the opposite, in fact. I may well be his biggest disappointment," I comment with a sigh but hold my body rigid.

"Yet here you sit as Regent Major of North America," Walter Jackson says.

Silence blankets the room.

"By the majority vote of the Council," I remind them.

"As you say, my Regent," Kimberly responds, but there's a coldness in his gaze, and I suppress a shiver. "I understand you are dealing with a health crisis after your most recent encounter."

"It is the result of healing and the body's response."

"You know, pain and pleasure are but a touch apart. However, one must be able to touch another human to survive. I imagine it would be hard to experience pain at the mere thought of a lover's kiss. To never touch skin to skin in any meaningful way. For the words to fill your head in soft whispers as the images of all the things you need are right in front of you. Yet you know they will never be possible. The submissive side of your make-up needs consistency, touch and follow through. Without those things the structure crumbles and how long before you withdraw? Your Consort watching from the sidelines as you become nothing, right in front of his eyes. You asked why Edmund might attack you? You rejected him, my Regent, and ran into the arms of another man. How much rejection is anyone supposed to take before they break?" Kimberly says, his tone icy but smooth on the surface.

"I'm not a monster. It would never have worked between Edmund and me," I comment as my mind races through his words.

"We are all the villain in someone else's story. It looks like you're the villain in his," he replies.

I shake my head to clear my thoughts. The papers on my desk become an odd blur as I try to focus a thought which won't quite take shape. I stare down until the words come into focus.

"Mr. Michaels, don't you have a substantial investment in a medical laboratory?" I ask without raising my gaze.

"It is not a hidden fact, Regent," Kimberly says, exuding calmness.

"It is odd that a former member of your house attacked me and injected me with an unknown substance."

"Are you accusing me of something?"

"It's a simple question of the conjunction of situations, wouldn't you say?"

"On the surface, it seems to be a simple conclusion based on a lack of intellectual prowess," he replies. "Which would explain why so many wanted you in the Regent's seat."

The words make a direct hit to my emotions. It takes every ounce of self-control I have to sit still and not give it away.

"Then you won't mind if I convene a formal investigation into your lab," I say and meet his hard gaze.

"We are at your service," he replies and nods.

"Good, let's make sure it stays that way," I reply and stand.

Everyone in the room follows my lead and rises from their chairs.

"Thank you both for coming today, and for your cooperation in the upcoming inquires," I say as a way of dismissal.

"It is our pleasure to serve you, my Regent. Even if you weren't our choice," Kimberly Michaels says without lowering his gaze.

"Next time you want to call us in for a talk with the principal, girl, make sure you have a reason," Walter Jackson sneers. "My Regent."

"I look forward to working with you both and hope, as we move forward, we will all find common ground for the greater good."

Both men make a slight bow, and I motion to the door.

I hold my body rigid as they walk across my office. The minute the door shuts, I lower myself into my chair and release a heavy sigh.

"I can't do this," I comment out loud as I close my eyes, forgetting Reece is sitting in the chair on the right side of my office.

"You can and you will," he says with a soft growl.

His voice startles me, and my eyes fly open in search for him.

"They hate me. For all I know, they want me dead. Both of them hold high positions in court, and I need them on my side to get anything done."

"Does anyone on your staff, here at the club or in any of your other situations, dislike you?" Reece asks.

"Of course. I'm sure people don't like the decisions I've made or the direction I've taken things. No one will like you a hundred percent of the time," I reply and shrug.

"How is this different?"

"I haven't been in this job long enough to be loathed. They hate me by association."

"Welcome to politics. They'll hate you by association, held beliefs, because you won... it doesn't matter. This is the position. You need to learn how use the power of both sides of you, rather than trying to bulldoze through it like a male Dominant. You have a different tool-box-use it!"

"What the hell do you want from me?" I scream in frustration. "Look at me! I can't be touched, I don't have a damn clue what I'm doing, and everything inside is..."

"Is what?" he asks with an eerie calmness.

"Scared. Out of balance. Weak! I can't figure out how to lift these worlds anymore," I spit.

"Careful," Reece warns.

"Or what? You'll touch me? Great! The world is trying to touch me. People want me to solve problems while others want me dead. It doesn't matter what I need-if I give in to anything but being a Dominant like all that other 'domly dom' bullshit, then I am the weak one. They've made the playing field, I just have to use their rules."

"That is not the Atlas I know," he says.

"Well, it is the weak-ass Atlas you've got."

Muscles tense across my body, and I fight my response to the pain.

"Weakness is not accepting the help or perspective you need," Reece replies.

"I don't know what I need."

"Yes you do, you've just cut it off for so long you don't know how to use all of you in harmony."

"I don't know how to get there from here," I say with resignation.

"That is why it is an exchange. It is why both of us can't lead at the same time. This is your domain. It is my domain to make sure you grow stronger. A place where only my structure matters, no matter how the rest of your world is held together. I am where you ask for help in every way, so we can move mountains together."

I shake my head. "I don't know what that looks like," I reply and stretch my neck.

"Yes you do. It means being able to move between ruling the world and following under my rule, at the same time, as well as when you need to park the world."

REECE WATCHES ME FROM HIS CHAIR. HIS EYES FOLLOW AS I resettle behind my desk.

"Don't sit down. Place your palms flat on the desk but don't put your weight on them," he says.

I stare at him until he raises an eyebrow, then I lean forward and place my hands flat on the desk. Pain lights through my skin, and I move until it subsides.

"Now that is sexy as hell," he says as he rises from his chair and walks over toward the desk until he is positioned beside me. His breath grazes across my ear.

"When we solve this little medical mystery of yours, this is one of several positions with which you will become familiar. For a while, you'll know the possibility is coming because your outfit will include a floor-length skirt rather than pants. Every meeting will challenge you, because I know clothes are your armor, but all armor has vulnerabilities."

He doesn't move. My breath quickens with each word, and the world shifts ever so slightly.

"When you've been especially difficult, or I deem it desirable or necessary, you may walk into your office and see a small bowl of kumquats. Each passing moment will ramp your anticipation. It won't matter if I am holding an audience with you or off with duties on my schedule. You'll know that at some point you'll be told to place the kumquat in your mouth and assume this, or another, position. No matter what happens to you, the expectation is that the kumquat remains in your mouth unharmed. You may not spit it out and crushing it will bring consequences. No matter how long the situation may last, until the command is given to consume it, you must hold it in place unharmed, knowing I may call for an inspection at any time. Since there's a bowlful, upon consumption, it may very well start things over or I may take our game to a new level."

Everything in me tries to block out the image and embrace its perfection in the same breath.

"Maybe, underneath the long skirt, there are panties and maybe there are none. The door of the office might be locked, or your assistant could walk in at any second to announce your next appointment. Or, in the darkness of night, you'll be lashed to a balcony rail, where you may be clothed or stripped to face the swirl of your fears and desires," he says without raising his voice.

"Either way, whether by physical restraint or by command, your hands will not move. However, mine will lift the edge of your skirt with an appreciative slowness. I will see every hitch of your breath, feel your pulse thud underneath your skin, and watch the shiver race along your spine. I may take the edge of the fabric and tuck it into the waistband at the small of your back, exposing you to me, but easily covering if the world necessitates."

I close my eyes and fight for control as my teeth clench.

"A tight jaw would ruin a kumquat," he reminds.

I force my jaw to relax. Muscles throughout my body ripple in effort, setting off small sparks of pain, but my mind is so overwhelmed with the imagery I barely notice.

"In this position, your tight little pucker is framed by the fabric of your skirt. You might hear the snap of a glove, the rip of a condom, or me preparing a toy. The delicious licks of desire will wrap around you in every way while you await my choice. It is the helplessness, the anticipation, the giving up control while fighting against it. You are gorgeous in this state, but intoxicating when all those things evaporate. The release of your world into my hands when you hold on to no more control than the amount I allow."

With a hard swallow, I shift my body to find a mental and emotional toe hold.

"Don't move. Here I own you. I will possess you in any way I choose, for both of our benefits. Your interaction with me will always be hierarchical because you thrive on a place of rules, structure, and a release of control. Some days I'll get you here with slow gentle seduction as I use your body, mind, and emotions to paint the path for you. Other times, I'll kick the pedestal right out from under you and watch you deal with a primal fear, just like I did the other day when I used the pain of your body against you."

I lick my lips. My mouth is dry. Everything in me wants to beg, but I don't know for what. It is exquisite.

"It is possible I'll shove a syringe full of lube inside that tight little pucker of yours, preparing it for my finger to slowly fuck you until your arousal drips down your thighs. Then, perhaps, I'll work a plug deep in your ass and return you to work, letting you know that you'll be returned to a similar position that evening. Then I will fuck you hard, but not fast, holding my entire length in you as your muscles grab and release. My fingers pinching your taut hard nipples, or maybe I'll place two magnetic balls on them as I enjoy the pleasurable pain rippling through you. Perhaps I will take you in every hole you've got available or put you into an intellectual predicament to hold you right below the ability to let go."

"Please." The word startles me as it leaves my lips in a hoarse whisper.

"Please what, pet? Touch you, fuck your body, play with your mind, give you the structure and consequence which let you grow but give you hard expectations to lift the burden from you? For what do you beg?"

I nod.

"Yes." I force the word out.

Reece chuckles lightly against my ear.

"Oh, my dear. We are just getting started. I will never tire of such an exquisite creature. Finding new ways to torture you and nurture you. Thrusting you over uncomfortable edges until they become comfortable and then find new ones to do it all again."

Tears form, but I blink them back.

"What if you can never touch me?" I choke on the words.

"Do you feel pain right now?"

I pull my awareness back into my body and realize while the pain exists, it is not overwhelming. The weight of Reece's hand sits lightly on my lower back, and the tears spill.

A knock at the door barely draws my attention.

"Ma'am, your two o'clock appointment is here," Katie announces.

I lift my head and look over at her. Her face bunches in concern as she looks between Reece and me.

"Is everything okay, Ma'am?"

With a deep breath, I nod.

"Please prepare some tea and an assortment of small sandwiches from the kitchen," Reece says. "And show Dr. White into the office."

"Yes, Mr. Gabriel," she replies, confusion tingeing her tone.

My head snaps, and I look over at Reece as I attempt to stand up.

"I didn't give you permission to move," he comments.

"This is my office, and I didn't know I was expecting Dr. White."

"Yes. It is your office, but I made the appointment. I thought he might help provide some temporary relief to your current situation."

I scowl at Reece, but don't move my hands.

Katie clears her throat as she enters the room.

"Dr. White," Reece says from his leaning position on my desk. "Please, have a seat."

Across the room, Katie closes the door with a click.

"How did it go?" he asks as he moves into the room.

"Better than expected," Reece replies. "Take a seat, Atlas. Thank you for coming, Jacob."

I rise from my position and jerk down my jacket. The move is immediately met with searing pain. Aggravation flairs through me, and I cringe.

"My Regent." Jacob White makes a slight bow. "How may I be of service?"

CHAPTER TWENTY

"Dr. White," I acknowledge and take my seat. Across from me, he waits for my acknowledgment.

I'm internally caught between two worlds. The outward expectation, as Regent, sits in juxtaposition with the head space Reece lured me into accepting.

Reece looks over and gives me a knowing half smile and walks to take his seat beside Dr. White. When he stands in front of the chair, I nod to both of them, and they take a seat.

"I apologize for being caught unaware," I say, looking over at Reece. "A situation I'll rectify in the future, but I did not know you'd requested an appointment to see me."

"He didn't," Reece answers. "Jacob and I have talked several times since our first meeting in the hallway. He's a world-class hypnotherapist, though his hobbies are more entertaining."

"I'm glad you are finding 'friends' within your new world," I say with a flatness that shows my lack of patience.

"Based on his work with chronic pain management, I believe he may be able to offer relief until we find alternative solutions, my Regent," Reece says as he levels a harsh gaze at me.

"I'm listening."

"How much do you know about hypnosis, Regent?" Jacob asks.

"More than the masses, not enough to be a hypnotist."

"Good, because we can hit the highlights and move on to how I may help."

I nod.

"Many people think the state of hypnosis is where you lose control. A place where someone else tells you what to do and you follow without awareness. In fact, hypnosis is a place where we give you more control. There, you can follow the suggestion or refuse. Your mind won't ever let you cross a hard moral boundary, but it will let you go into an area where you would normally hold back. While the conscious mind filters your daily inputs, it is believed the subconscious mind is a more efficient processing center because it takes things in without the filters. Most of the time, the conscious mind passes the information off, but there are certain states we enter where the subconscious mind is front and center because we've turned off the conscious one," he explains.

"What does this have to do with pain management?" I ask.

Jacob chuckles when Reece lets out a deep sigh.

"It's a good question, which I'll return with one of my own. When I walked in, Reece had his hand on your lower back. Did his touch hurt?"

I shake my head. "No."

"Yet when you pulled down sharply on your jacket to move your mental state back to a different place, the pain was searing."

For a long moment I stare at him. It is unnerving to hear the depth of his observation.

"No, Regent, I am not magical," he says and chuckles. "Not only did I have foreknowledge, I knew what to look for when I walked into your office. Don't get me wrong; I observe everything, and our conversations would reveal more than you're used to, but in this case... I had a head start."

Confusion radiates in waves off of me, and I scowl.

"Mr. Gabriel came to me with great concern for your well-being after the incident. I was cleared by the Council to consult. They hoped the pain would subside on its own, but recent revelations are proving the opposite is true. So I am consulting on your case."

"Good to know I'm a case now," I say as I roll my eyes. I can almost hear Reece growl his response, but the room is silent.

"For the last few days, we've worked to see if hypnosis was possible. To know if at the most basic level, it would achieve any level of results."

"And your conclusion, Dr. White?"

"Did you feel pain on your back when the Consort touched you?" Jacob shoots back.

The question's directness startles me. It isn't couched in etiquette for my position, but a bluntness to make his point. I smile.

"No, Doctor, I did not. Until he brought it to my attention."

"Did you feel aroused?"

I bite my lip out of habit and immediately release it with an internal reprimand.

"I'll take that as a yes. The emotions you felt and the focused path of the Consort's words helped you move to the necessary space for release. Your desire for what he said, in addition to the fact he was leading, allowed your critical mind to step out of the way and your subconscious to take the words at face value. This is the essence of hypnosis. The ability to go from a wide view to a singular point. There, the mind can ignore some signals and amplify others," Jacob says with a smile.

"Wait, you're saying Reece used hypnosis?"

"The essence of it. He provided a situation which off balanced you and then redirected your thoughts to where you've already offered him power. Your mind had no reason not to trust his intentions; therefore, you followed the imagery in his words. Part of you, at a minimum, wants to be in that space. Since that is true, there was no resistance. The body shifted to a state of desire and arousal and away from the chronic pain which plagues you. With practice, you may find you can reduce your pain for longer and longer periods of time with the technique, along with medical assistance."

"So what I'm hearing is that my pain is all in my mind."

"Quite the opposite, Regent. I am saying your mind is your greatest weapon, even against pain."

"I could use a few of those," I say with a smirk.

"Regent, you command an army of people who, by your position alone, will follow you and give you any resource you deem necessary. All you need to do is realize it's all in your hands and stop running," Jacob says.

His words strike a chord. I've been playing defense so long I didn't take the time to realize the surrounding people had worked me into a position of offense.

"Thank you, Dr. White," I say as I rise from my chair. "I look forward to working with you."

Both men stand, and Jacob gives me a slight bow.

"Please let me know how I may be of service, my Regent," he says and walks to the door.

"Welcome back to the game, Atlas," Reece says and smiles.

"Guess it's time to show them what it looks like when they decide to play with me," I reply with a confident grin.

CHAPTER TWENTY-ONE

Two days later, my security detail gathers in the studio apartment over the PR firm. They have transformed the seating area with a large conference table surrounded by office chairs. Portable whiteboards dominate the end near the window in an arc. Words, colors, lines, circles, and erasure marks cascade out from Kimberly, Edmund, and Walter's names. Their pictures sit in the corner of their respective boards. It is an awe-inspiring sight as I watch them work from the kitchen bar. As long as I stay on this side of the apartment, they work easily in a casual manner. Ideas are yelled from one end of the table to the other. Across the floor, a bright blue tape line gives the visual boundary. It wouldn't matter if I told them to stand down; the minute I step across it, the entire mood changes.

If I'd stayed in the confines of the Sovereign Society, this would be a less foreign environment. Dominick would have changed my training as soon as the Council decided upon my appointment, and most likely before, in hopes of my elevation to the position. Instead, I did the one thing no one anticipated and walked away. While I wouldn't have changed my experiences for anything, it puts me a few steps behind in every direction I turn.

Reece walks out of the bedroom as he puts his phone in his pocket. The absence of his cane draws my immediate attention when he leans in and brushes a kiss across my forehead.

"I see your work with Jacob has yielded some results," I remark without taking my eyes off the chaos on the other side of the room.

"Yours as well. It is nice to be able to touch in the lightest way, though I want to do so much more to you," Reece replies, and I watch his head turn, from my periphery, to follow my gaze.

"Is everything okay in your 'other world'?"

"Within reason. My sister is concerned I dropped off the grid, though I reminded her I was nearly killed recently and felt it was best to take some time to reflect on my world."

I snort and cover my mouth in embarrassment.

"How's the reflection going, my Consort?"

"I'll let you know when we catch the SOB who tried to kill us," he says with a sense of gravity.

"Shall we go make order out of chaos?"

"Do you have a plan based on what they know?" Reece asks with a nod toward the crowd across the room.

"My plans have plans," I quip.

"Not lately," he returns.

I sigh. "True. I went up a level, and I wasn't quite as prepared as I thought."

"The first step is to admit you have a problem," Reece volleys.

"Maybe my problem is my Consort. He can be an asshole at times."

"Careful, girl," he says, lightly teasing.

I laugh and set down the glass of water I've been sipping.

"Well, there's no time like the present. It doesn't look like we completely lack information on the suspects based on the information on those boards, although it is thin. Still, we've got to move on something. I refuse to hide out any longer, and they have told me I've got an army at my back, on multiple occasions. Let's see if the mobiliza-tion of said army has yielded any results," I say as I straighten.

"As you command, my Regent," Reece says with a light bow.

"It's time to show them how this game will really go," I say and step around the bar.

I stride across the tape line, and all conversation immediately ceases. Everybody in the room comes to immediate attention, and I smile.

"Tell me what you've got, Garrett, and do not disappointment," I say as I take a seat at the head of the table.

"Please be seated," I comment and watch Garrett walk toward the boards at the other end of the table.

Around me, chairs scrape across the floor, papers rustle, and keyboards click. The projector in the middle of the table comes on and projects an image onto the only clean board. Beside me, Reece pulls a chair to my right side.

Garrett nods toward me and then turns to see the makeshift screen.

"Kimberly Michaels owns a medical laboratory. They are under contract for seven different pharmaceutical companies with over fifty-three drug trials, six research projects, and two military contracts, which are classified. In addition, he owns two small side business which look to be run by previous contractees. There's no doubt he's a shrewd businessman, and without looking deeper into his company, we can't definitively prove his involvement," Garrett says.

I nod for him to continue.

"Those two smaller businesses have some connections to Walter Jackson, who owns a marketing firm. They are his clients but in the grander scale are of no import. Edmund's current busi-ness conglomerations are more complex. In the past two years he's bought several small or start-up companies, stripped them for their assets and intellectual property, then assimilated them or sold them off, either as more efficient companies or assets only. He's very successful in this kind of business flipping. In his current portfolio, there is a small academically sponsored lab running two pain management trials, but their results are not positive. The rest of the portfolio is a mix of IT, security, junk start-ups, and three hydroponic farms."

"Is there a connection to either Kimberly Michaels or Walter Jackson and Edmund?" I ask.

"Outside of the connection of his contracts and original training, we've not yet found a connection."

"Did you say contracts, plural?"

Garrett nods.

"Before his last contract, he served a two-year contract for Walter Jackson. The House of the Rising Star trained him to be a financial advisor and business consultant. Edmund's acumen was exceptional, and Mr. Jackson's marketing company direly needed process and fiscal improvement, as he's a spendthrift."

"What was Mr. Jackson's debt load in the past two years?" I ask with a frown.

In the middle of the table, the click of a computer keyboard echoes off the walls. Garrett frowns at the woman who stares at the screen in front of her.

"It has moved from more than a sixty percent debt to income ration to five percent," she reports without looking up.

"How fast did that drop happen?" Kade asks.

"In a period of six months," she replies.

"I presume this red flag is on the board somewhere," I ask as I raise an eyebrow.

"We are still looking through the financials," Garrett responds.

"We are in the middle of a crisis. Still looking at... doesn't cover it. You're in DC. Every investigation in this town is based on how well you can be blackmailed. Why the hell wasn't this one of the first threads?" I demand. "Make it an action item. You said Edmund owned three hydroponic farms?"

"Yes, Ma'am."

"Why? Is he trying to find a cure for world hunger?"

"We presumed they were flips he picked up and hadn't turned over yet."

"Hydroponic farms are great on a small scale. They are efficient for estates and those who want to be self-sufficient but aren't commercially viable on a larger scale. In other words, they can feed a family or a specific business but can't sustain enough profit for anything larger. Which means it makes little sense for anyone to buy them and flip them. Unless it is used for cannabis production, which makes them much more viable, but still...Where did you say those farms were located?"

Garrett flips through the papers in front of him.

"Colorado," he replies.

"That might explain it. He thought the market would explode. It's made good strides but not the explosion everyone was hoping," I say with a sigh. "Based on this, we're nowhere. So much for the army of intel. My own knowledge could get us this far."

"Condescending doesn't look good on you, Atlas," Kade says from his position in the middle of the table.

"And you don't look good in not knowing what the hell is going on, Kade."

"This from a woman who nearly got herself killed in her own club because she wouldn't listen to her security," he shoots back.

There's a collective gasp around the room.

"Touché. Too bad that security did not know there was a hidden doorway in my 'secure' panic room."

"Well, you've put your security running chase since the beginning of this whole situation."

"So you believe this whole mess to be my fault?" I say with calmness.

"If the shoe fits," he replies.

"And, does it? Does the shoe of blame lay all on my shoulders? I'm glad to carry the weight, as my namesake suggests, but you'd better be right."

Kade runs a hand through his hair and sighs. "Why did he come to the club and request you that first time? Why you? There were three other female Dominants on staff, but he requested you specifically. When he was told there was a wait list, and you were booked, he tripled the fee to get on your list. He paid the listed fee to the club and the rest to you in a tip. You lost two clients the month you took him on. Why?" he asks.

"I don't know. The club had been open... what... right under a year? I was lowering my client list because it, and my other endeavors, were taking so much time. So the loss of two clients wasn't unusual or unwelcome at that point."

"But all he wanted to do was serve you. Wait on you hand and foot? Impress you with gifts?"

I scowl as the information moves through my thoughts. There is something we are all missing. The question is what?

CHAPTER TWENTY-TWO

K ade's words turn in my mind until they consume every thought. Anger and vulnerability war with determination and strength. Months of running collide with the internal demand to stand my ground.

As the thoughts dissipate to a singular path, I smile. No one will like what I am about to say, but I know it is the right thing to bring this situation with Edmund to an end. There's more to this game, but if I can eliminate the pawn and work this problem, the rest will follow.

I slam my fist on the desk as clarity strikes and immediately regret it as pain shudders up my arm.

"You're right, Kade," I start. There's a collective gasp around the room, and all eyes turn toward him. "I've been running this entire time. At every turn, I've given in to fear when all Edmund wanted to do was serve me. We should let him."

"What?" Reece demands from my right.

"No!" Garrett says in unison from the other end of the table.

"Brilliant, Ma'am," Kade replies with a smile on his face. "Risky, but brilliant."

Murmurs fill the room, and I smile to myself.

"You can't be serious!" Garrett says as he paces in front of the boards. "He tried to kill you last time he got near you."

I shake my head.

"No. He was playing all sides of the game," I reply. "I assure you, if he wanted me dead, I'd be dead."

"Regent, I know you've been under tremendous stress as of late, but..."

I raise my hand to end Garrett's protest and rise from my chair. Around me, everyone follows until the room is silent.

"Keep digging. You all are missing something. There's a game going on, and we are missing the moves with this distraction. You're supposed to be the best Obsidian Overwatch has at its disposal. Prove it."

With a slight flourish, I step away from the table and start walking toward the bedroom.

"Consort, Garrett, Kade... with me please," I say without turning around.

Behind me, Garrett growls out orders, and two sets of footfalls start in my direction. I brace myself for the onslaught. No one will like my proposal. It is both beautiful in its simplicity and risky in its execution.

As I enter the bedroom, I assess the best position of power and head to the small seating area under the window. Reece has sat there vigilant on so many nights because it is the best view of the room.

The image floods me with desires and needs I must deny because of my physical state. I'm lucky he can touch me with the slightest caress, but I miss being held tight or pinned in place. There's so much to be said for being able to transition between two different states.

I sit down in the chair and tuck my foot behind my ankle, letting the nerves spike and numb by their own over excitement. Moments later, Reece walks through the door, surveys the room, and shoots me a glare when he finds me. The look on my face tells me exactly what he's thinking, and none of it is happy. He continues in and sits down in the chair beside me.

Kade and Garrett walk in one right after the other. Each one is shooting daggers at the other with a look, and I stifle a laugh. All this male posturing would amuse at other times, but I know it is all about to land on me.

The door shuts with a slight shudder, and Kade winces a little at the result of his heavy hand. Both of them step into the sitting area and stand at parade rest.

Tense silence lingers in the air, and I use it to my advantage. No one can speak until I utter a word. Reece could blow my position, but his curiosity won't let him. It is a game of chess between us. I revel in each move, both to my advantage and my detriment.

"None of you are to speak until I am done. You will hear me out in completion and remember your own places before you remind me of mine," I say and take a deep breath.

Kade shifts his weight with the slightest movement. A micro expression creases Garrett's brow. I don't look over at Reece because I already know his incoming reaction. Besides, watching the two in front of me entertains me enough to continue.

"While out of line in his presentation, Kade was right in his assessment. The immediate problem lies in the distraction Edmund has provided, but I don't think he's part of the larger game. There's an underlying power struggle within the Society. I know it's obvious, but better to apply words to it than let it go as an assumption," I say with a wave of my hand in dismissal of my words.

"However, we need to remove the pawn from the board to see the greater game. To that end, I believe it best to go back where all of this started. I will invite Edmund to serve me once again. A place where we can start fresh and remove the cloud of various issues and under-standings. Maybe I am wrong, but I think Edmund is being manipu-lated more than he is manipulating. At his base level, I think he wants to serve, but the needs are so deep and abused in various ways that he acts out. He carries significant power in the greater world by his sheer monetary clout, but such weight can be a burden to a submissive soul."

Beside me, Reece almost growls his displeasure while Garrett opens his mouth, and Kade shakes his head. I hold up my hand to stop their objections before they are expressed.

"Yes. It is a dangerous set of assumptions. Based on more of the board being uncovered in recent weeks, I believe someone pressured him into driving me away from my support system. My weakness and belief that everyone is my responsibility was a well-played strategy. Every insecurity pushed until they consumed me. I don't think anyone believed I would reach out to Dominick."

"You can't be serious!" Reece explodes.

"Quite," I say with a calmness I do not internalize.

"Edmund tried to kill you, Regent. He carved his initial into your chest. You can't move or be touched without pain. How could you even think he's a victim in all of this?" Garrett says.

Kade remains silent, but a hint of a smile plays on the edge of his mouth.

"Every person has a point where they will do whatever they think it takes to protect those which are important to them. Even if the actions hurt," I reply.

"So what are you proposing? That your bait? You call Edmund up and offer to let him serve you like nothing ever happened?" Reece asks as he stands and paces in a line beside the sitting area.

"Yes. Do whatever you all feel is best to provide the protection in which you are comfortable. Turn on cameras. Post people outside once he walks into the room. I don't care, but I don't want him harmed, nor do I want anyone else in the room."

"This is insane," Reece spits.

"Probably, but we aren't getting anywhere on our current path."

"Ma'am," Kade says.

I look up at him and raise an eyebrow.

"Why?"

I shrug and watch three pairs of eyes turn their stares toward me.

"Call it a hunch. Needs can drive humans to do crazy things for the hint or hope that it might fulfill them."

"Are you willing to risk your life on a hunch?" Garrett asks.

"I am."

"Even if it is not yours to risk?" Reece counters.

"Yes. The problem with being Regent is that I serve the greater good first and everything else second, including you, my Consort. However, it also means I have one of the best protective teams in the world. You don't have to like the idea, but it is your responsibility to implement it with all due care."

"I, most definitely, dislike this idea," Garrett says. Beside him, Reece huffs his agreement.

"Enjoying yourself, Kade?" I ask.

"Yes, Ma'am."

"Care to share with the rest of the class?"

"I was thinking how good it is to have you back and curious what you think the end game is here?"

"I believe delving into Mr. Michaels' and Mr. Jackson's perspectives, motives, and gains is a good place to start."

"If you think this is all true, why would he want you to hurt?" Reece stops pacing and looks at me again.

"He didn't want to kill me, but he wanted my attention. Pain can focus people because they want to avoid it or embrace it. If my guess is close, he thought it would take me out but not 'take me out.' Someone is playing on his deep internal needs. We think people will always act rationally in moments of personal crisis, but rarely is that the case. As I well proved."

"And if you're wrong?" Kade asks.

"Then you all better be there to save my dumb ass. It is the job you signed up for, you know," I say with a smile.

"This is insanity," Reece says as he leans against the wall.

"Yes," I agree without elaboration.

"You don't think you can call him up, and he'll come like a lost puppy, do you?" Garrett asks.

I shake my head. "No. I figured I'd call a truce. He knows I can't be his, but this world of ours doesn't take pieces off the board because they've found their 'mate.' Look at Samantha; she has several partners of different varieties. It isn't impossible to believe my dominant side would want a submissive to serve me. There is something delicious about watching someone who kneels before you. I won't lie and tell any of you I don't miss it at times. Most of the time my other responsibilities fill in such things until I am overwhelmed by them, but nothing can replace that which passes between a Dominant and submissive."

"Indeed," Reece says in agreement.

"You don't think he'll turn on you?" Kade asks.

I shrug. "He might. There's no way to know, but I am a damn good Dominant, both personally and professionally. Before you ask, that's arrogance, not cockiness-I can back it up."

Kade chuckles. "Yes, Ma'am. You can back it up without a doubt," he confirms.

I smile up at him.

"The club will require the lock to be useless. We will switch all cameras and audio in the room on with full monitoring. A minimum of three club security personnel will be in the area at all times. Whatever Obsidian Overwatch wants to provide from that point is up to them," Kade says and looks over at Garrett.

"Wait. You're going along with this? Do you not understand her new position?" Garrett shoots back.

"I know you're new around here, and your position trumps mine because of an elevated position in this Society thing, but you need to learn a thing or two about the woman sitting before you. While you've caught her in one of her lowest lows, she is a force of nature. Her stubbornness will not only wear you down, but you'll wonder what the hell happened if you don't do as she wishes. When she's decided something, you can help, hold on, or get out of the way. Personally, I've found over the years, it is better to help," Kade replies.

"This is insane! For all we know, he plans to kill you, and after his little stunt the last time, might succeed this time," Garrett says and breaks his position.

"It isn't actually insane. For the first time we are controlling the variables, rather than letting them control us. From the moment he dropped to his knee and asked me to marry him, my every action has been reactionary. We can't... I can't keep stepping back on the defense. The only way to gain power over the Council is to take care of this situation. If something this... small, in the grander sense, is going to bamboozle us, then I might as well quit now."

"Consort, please help here." Garrett turns to Reece.

"No. Kade's right, as is Atlas. I don't like it, but there's no doubt we need to turn this situation around. Someone, somewhere is behind something bigger. If not, then wiping this piece from the board makes for smooth sailing. However, I want to add Dominick's household to the investigation," Reece says.

"Why?" I ask as I try to keep my voice neutral.

"Things don't make sense. There are things Mr. Michaels and Mr. Jackson would not know. I'd investigate Kade, but my preliminary inquiries speak far too highly of him, as well as his protectiveness."

"Thanks. I think," Kade replies as he cocks his head and scowls.

"Let's not forget, Dominick put Cassandra here. Based on what I've learned, she caused some havoc. I don't know if it was malicious or misguided, but I think it best if we check out all such anomalies."

"Dominick has always had my best interest in mind," I counter.

"Be that as it may, Atlas, if you want my support for what is a near suicidal plan on paper, then you will acquiesce to my request without further discussion," Reece says as he gives me a withering look.

I sigh as I battle internally to hold my ground.

"As you wish, my Consort. You'll find him to be above reproach."

"For your sake, I hope you are correct, but is his household?" he asks and turns toward Garrett. "We must trust you because you are her assigned protective detail, and paranoia will not serve this situation well. But if you place one toe out of line, I will presume you are part of the game, and the attention will turn to you. Until Dominick is cleared, you are suspicious by association."

"Unfair though such may be?" Garrett says.

"Prove your loyalty and honor, then I will welcome you into the Regent's household by your actions, not on the word of those I do not know," Reece replies.

"Okay. Now that you boys have sprayed testosterone all over my room in a 'my dick is bigger than yours' contest, let's get down to business. Shall we?"

The room goes silent as the three men turn toward me.

"If you ever need help knocking her down a peg or two, once I've proven myself to you, I do hope you'll call me, Consort. Such would be quite the pleasure," Garrett says without taking his gaze off me.

"I'll keep that in mind," Reece says.

"I told her she needed to be knocked down every once in a while," Kade chimes in.

I scowl at the three of them, and all of them return the look with a smirk.

"Gentlemen, if you are quite done, I will remind you of my due respect," I say as I lift my chin.

"We are at your command," Garrett says.

Then, in almost perfect unison, the three bow slightly at the waist.

"My Regent," they reply.

I sigh. "Every one of you better be glad I like you. Now let's get down to business, shall we?" I say with a shake of my head.

CHAPTER TWENTY-THREE

A week later, I sit in Alexandra's dressing room and stare at my reflection. My entire world is different. The person staring back at me isn't the one who started this chaotic journey. I am unsure what to make of my world and yet, here I sit once again transforming into the outer persona in which I draw my power. Every person in the world wears a mask, but I've taken it to a new level.

I shift on the stool, and pain ripples through me. It is a near constant companion, but the hypnosis has helped.

With a deft movement, I apply eye shadow across my lids. The contour sinks them in and makes the look harsher. Each hard line and contour adds to the effect until I don't recognize myself.

My stomach churns as the clock on the wall ticks down the seconds as I replay the conversation which brought me to this point.

Three days ago, I dialed Edmund's number. A room full of people watched as I talked to him.

"Well, well, well. This was not a call I was expecting to receive," Edmund said as he answered the phone.

"Hello, Edmund."

"I know you aren't calling to tell me you are leaving the Regent position and your chosen Consort. So to what do I owe the honor of this call?"

"Edmund, I want to call a truce. When I refused your proposal, it wasn't meant to hurt you or reject you. There's nothing I can say to make you feel differently; only you can feel what you feel. But I would like to talk. Face to face," I said with steady confidence as I closed my eyes and remembered his last session.

He laughed.

"You want me to walk willingly into an obvious trap? Surrounded by those who claim to protect you while they throw you at the Society?"

"I am asking you to come talk to me. Under my command, were you ever in a position where you did not feel safe?"

There was a long silence, and I braced for his answer.

"No," Edmund replied.

"Then on my word and honor as a Dominant, I promise no harm will come to you so long as you willingly fall under my command. All commands. I want to know how this all went wrong."

"Are you naïve or stupid, Regent?" he spat.

"Probably both," I replied.

"I'm sure it will please your Council to know such. Under your reign, if that is the case, their power will increase tenfold."

"Indeed."

"What? No power play?"

"I see no reason. You are in control of the situation. In your hands, my world has been destroyed more than once. My Consort hobbled and my body enveloped in pain at the slightest touch. In a game of chess, we'd be in the final moves, but victory is much sweeter without haste and in person."

"You make an eloquent argument, my dear spider."

"I didn't threaten you with thermonuclear war on your life. You did on mine and delivered it well. At every turn I've been on the back foot. If I am to admit defeat, then I would prefer to do it in person," I said.

"If I step into your club, we both know I won't step out of it under my own power."

"I can guarantee, as long as I remain safe that you will remain the same. Are you not curious to know what it feels like to kneel at my feet one last time before you declare your victory, boy?"

His shuddered breath echoed through the phone.

"You were always a temptress."

"And you were always one of my favorites. To watch you serve me with grace and elegance was one of my deepest pleasures. No one, in my present or past, ever came close to such a level. You could read my desires by the smallest motions. I miss our power exchange dance."

"As do I," Edmund said. The tone of his voice softened, and I relaxed a little.

"Then we should dance one last time. Let this battle of pain and suffering be done between us. Declare your victory, so we may both find a path forward," I coaxed.

"You know they will never let me out of there."

"Trust my control. Of all the things in my world, my control over it is the one thing I have not lost."

"Do you really believe that?"

"Yes."

"Then I would watch the knives of those in your court, Regent. Enemies often look as friends and friends often look as enemies."

"Indeed."

"Give me your promise and your word of my safety," Edmund said.

"You have my promise that under my command you will be safe. You have my word that I will honor all which was said here between us."

"Three days from now. Seven pm," he said.

"You'll be escorted to my private room. The one where we were last in session."

"As you wish, Ma'am."

The line went dead.

Now I sit and stare at my reflection. The clock behind my head reads six-thirty. In thirty minutes, I will face Edmund once again. In my mind there are only two outcomes, though I worked to convince everyone around me of all the variables.

Ultimately, either I am right in my hunch, and he'll talk to me, or I am going to my death.

"You don't have to do this, you know," Reece says from behind me.

"We both know I do. One way or another, this needs to end," I say and force a smile.

"There's no way you can think he will fold."

I spin on the stool until I face Reece.

"At this moment, I don't know what to think. When this started, I was on the edge of burnout. My worries consisted of juggling a writing career, keeping Samantha on the road at book signings, and trying to run a vanilla public relations firm on the grounds of a BDSM club. All while moonlighting as a female Dominant and club owner. On paper, it sounds like an impossibility, but I was surrounded by a team of people dedicated to each area. They were passionate, smart, and made me look good. Then I fell off the edge and now my world looks nothing like when it started. What was up is down and what was down is up."

"I can't lose you, Atlas," Reece says.

"Then I'll try my best to come out the other side."

"You know, I'll never get over how much you transform. It's no wonder I missed the fact you and Alexandra were the same person. You look stunning in that latex outfit."

I laugh softly. "Thank you. I have to say I don't miss that constant transformation process, but it was easier because I've had some amazing teachers along the way. Each one left their mark. I am lucky so many of them crossed my path."

"Just for the record, I don't like this situation at all," Reece says as he crosses his arms over his chest.

"Your constant personal objection is noted, Consort. Thank you for supporting me publicly."

"I'll always have your back, and your front," he says and gives me a half grin.

"I can't wait to be under your command in every way you desire."

"Enough not to walk out there and do this crazy plan of yours?"

I shake my head. "How are the investigations coming along?"

"Nice change of subject," Reece says and raises an eyebrow. "The team is still compiling them. Every one of them has significant anomalies, either in their personal background or that of their household."

I scowl. "Even Dominick?"

Reece nods.

"Okay. Let's set up a review as soon as they are all compiled."

"As you wish," Reece replies.

I stand and walk over to him.

"Relax. Every protective detail in this place has my six."

"The last time you believed that, you almost died."

"Stop exaggerating. If Edmund wanted me dead, or you dead, we would be by now."

"According to the doctors, I would be if it weren't for your intervention," Reece says.

I shake my head to dissipate the memory on the boat.

"Doctors like to sound like heroes," I say and smile at him.

Reece sighs.

"Yes, I know. You don't like this plan, my Consort," I reply for him and lean forward to place a kiss on his cheek. "Stop worrying."

I step back and place my hand on the doorknob.

"Why does this feel like a goodbye?"

"Because you're watching my ass walk out this door," I whisper. "I'll see you soon. Kade's waiting for you in the command center."

"Come back to me, Atlas."

"You are home, Reece. I always return home, somehow."

I open the door and step out into the club. The click of my heels across the tile brings a rush of memories as I make my way to the room that will decide my fate.

CHAPTER TWENTY-FOUR

The club is a hive of activity. My entire team wanted to close it down for the night, but I vetoed the idea. It took a little leaning on the financials and forcing the issue based on my positions, but eventually they agreed.

My legs ache with each step. It's been weeks since I was in heels this high, but they give me a confidence which is hard to describe as I make my way through the club. The long black split skirt encircles my legs and floats up with each step. Every trick and skill I've learned is employed tonight. Without looking, I know each camera trails me through the club.

This used to be my world. The one place I came to hold my power. Here my word was final, but now I'm a figurehead while my real power sits in a world no one here knows exists. It is like stepping back into a life you didn't know you were leaving until it was gone.

With confident strides, I make my way over to the bar. The chill of the evening means the door to the pool area is down and shut. A small crush of bodies crowds the room. I take a moment and watch my former world with new eyes. My heart breaks a little, but I force a

SAPPHARIA MAYER

smile, not enough to remove my stern gaze but enough to let my wist-fulness out. In two more strides, I step up to the end of the bar.

The bartender pauses mid-wipe of the bar and stares at me.

"Good evening, Jack," I say without hesitation.

"Um... good evening, Alexandra... um, Ma'am," he stutters.

"A finger of Scotch, please."

"Uh... um... yes, Ma'am," Jack replies but doesn't move.

I raise an eyebrow, and Jack once against steps in motion. Around me, the level of conversation drops to hushed whispers. Seconds later, the glass of Scotch is set in front of me without a word.

"It got really quiet in here," I quip as I pick up the glass.

Jack nods, a dumbfounded look etched on his face.

"Any idea why?"

"You?"

"Me? I'm just another guest here this evening," I say then shoot the finger of Scotch. The warmth trail races down my throat, and I stifle the sigh of pleasure.

"Pardon me, um... Ma'am. You're a legend," Jack says as he leans in a little.

I chuckle and shake my head. "Legends are just stories people make up because they were too afraid to ask. I'm another person in this club looking good in latex."

"That is a fact. You look smoking. If it is okay for me to say that."

"Thank you. Now give me another shot of Scotch and I'll get out of everyone's hair."

"You know, I hear Alexandra doesn't like it when people drink right before they play, and in that get-up, I'm banking you're about to fuck someone up."

I wave my hand dismissively. "Alexandra's a bitch, and I'm too sweet to fuck someone up," I whisper conspiratorially.

Jack laughs without reserve, and all eyes turn toward us.

Without a doubt, I know displeasure is written all over my face because the looks don't last long. Seconds later, he slides a tall shot glass in front of me.

"Just don't tell her I served you," he whispers.

I nod my head toward the cameras. "I think the command center already knows and about right now, a couple of people are fuming, but don't worry-I'll protect you."

The color drains from Jack's face, and I chuckle.

"Always pay attention to your surroundings, Jack. A note of warning for later. For now, were you under my command when you served me?"

"Yes, Ma'am."

"Then you've got nothing to fear," I say and lift the glass in a salute toward the camera, then shoot it to the back of my throat. "Thank you, Jack. Now get back to the important people... our guests."

I nod my head toward the room and turn on my heel away from the bar.

Thoughts rush through me, but I push them away. I've done this walk hundreds of times. Tonight is no different, I tell myself. This is another session with Edmund, like all the ones before it.

WITH MEASURED STEPS, I MAKE MY WAY TO THE PLAYROOM. I want to take in each detail, but my emotions threaten to sweep me away.

The camera above me hums as it pans toward the door, and I look up. Behind the lens, half a dozen people watch every move I make. I lift my chin and stare straight into the camera, giving a wink and blowing a kiss. It reminds me of the day I met Reece as Alexandra and watched him walk through the club. When he looked up into the camera, I felt like he was looking right through me.

I take a deep breath and push open the playroom door. The lights are dim but only enough to take out the harsh glare. Without thought, I step into the room. On the counter to my right sits a bottle of Domaine de la Romanee-Conti La Tache 2010 with two wine glasses. I pause and tap the music icon on the control panel. The soft lilt of a cello fills the stifling silence.

The room is identical in every detail to the last time I sessioned with Edmund. It is a gamble. My anticipation is palpable as I step onto the dais. I run my hand across the arm of the baroque chair. The beautiful plush jewel encrusted sapphire velvet fabric intimidates me, knowing what the next minutes hold. My hand glides across the hand-carved wood; its size gives a sense of grandeur to the room. I beg my body for the surge of inner power, but I remain a mix of uncertainty and confidence as I lower myself into the chair. No matter what happens now, my fate is in my hands.

Across the room, the door opens, and I glance up at the clock as the second hand passes the twelfth position. Edmund is neither late nor early.

"You showed," he says as he steps into the room.

"So did you," I say without turning my gaze toward him. "I wasn't sure you were brave enough."

"How many eyes are watching our little tête-à-tête?"

"As many as you choose, I would presume. You know how to work the controls, boy," I say with forced confidence.

"Are you not scared to be alone with me, Alexandra? The last time we were face to face, let's just say... you suffered at my hands in ways which were unfathomable."

"Life is suffering. You've provided several such paths for me as of late."

The sound of the cork releasing from the wine bottle echoes softly around the room. I don't react, nor do I look toward the door. A slight clink of glass is the only notice before Edmund moves across the room as I watch him from my peripheral.

With practiced movements, he offers the tray toward me when he reaches the base of the dais. I lean forward and pick up the wineglass from the silver salver. The wine swirls in the glass as I move it without thought.

"Focus, Alexandra. You wouldn't want a drop of this exquisite wine to fall on your white carpet," he quips as he steps back and removes the other glass from the tray.

"Such would be a tragedy."

"It seems the tables are turned in our dance of power," he says with a haughty nod.

"Perhaps," I reply. "It is a commonly held belief that the submissive holds the power in an exchange by the nature of the exchange while the control is held by the Dominant. Though such is fluid depending on the relationship."

"And what if a person holds both the control and the power?" he asks with a raised brow.

"Then they call it abuse or ownership," I say with a tip of my glass toward him before bringing it to my lips and faking a sip.

"I see," Edmund says and follows my lead as he drains half of his glass.

"My team thinks I've lost my mind," I confide. "They believe you are here to kill me or incapacitate me. Though, for all intents and purposes, you've done the latter."

"How do you mean?"

"The drug you put in my system causes me constant pain. Every brush of the skin, every touch and every movement. It is the perfect sadistic weapon."

"It worked?" Surprise registers on his face.

"Don't act surprised. You knew exactly what you were doing the day you attacked me. Just like you knew what you were doing when you attacked Reece on the boat. Or even when you attacked your last contract owners."

"You know nothing, Alexandra. Though I was disappointed when Reece pulled through relatively unscathed," he said with an eerie calmness.

"Then enlighten me, Edmund," I reply.

"Why couldn't you just accept my proposal? I want to give you the world. There's more money at my disposal than I'll ever need. You would want for nothing."

I shake my head. "Why did you want Reece maimed?"

Edmund laughs but doesn't look up at me. "A Dominant is useless if they aren't in perfect health."

I raise an eyebrow. "Is that so? Then I'm no longer a Dominant, by your definition."

"True, but I can fix you," he says in a whisper.

"Speak up, boy; it is rude not to express yourself, so I can hear you," I press.

He lifts his glass and drains it then looks up at me. "Is there a reason you've barely touched your wine, Ma'am?"

"It is a trust issue. You turned my body against me, cut your initials into me, stalked me, stabbed Reece, poisoned the entire crew on the yacht... Do I need to continue?" I say with a shrug. "So you'll forgive me if I don't trust a glass of wine you poured."

"Would it be easier if I drank it to prove I came here in good faith?"

I nod. "It might be a good start," I say and offer him my glass.

He takes it without hesitation and drinks the wine in several long pulls. I stifle a smile and force my shoulders to relax.

"Now that we are on an even playing field, shall we begin?" I ask as confusion clouds his expression.

Edmund takes a step and stumbles, but rights himself. When he turns toward me too fast, he stumbles again. I watch with dispassion. There is neither pleasure nor anger as he struggles to comprehend his situation.

"I advise you sit or kneel, boy. It will make it easier," I say as I tuck my foot behind my ankle and lean forward in my chair with my elbows bracing against the arms.

In front of me, Edmund lunges toward me, but his legs give out, and he crashes to the floor.

"That's got to hurt," I quip as I watch him settle.

"Bitch," he says, the word coming out with a slight slur.

"I agree. My recent adventures taught me an important lesson. Those willing to harm others to obtain their goal will always win, unless their target levels the playing field and steps into the darkness. Welcome to my darkness."

I sit back and exhale the weight of my world. Power surges through me as I embrace my tumultuous emotions. Everything in me has tried to stay in the light while the darkness of the world demanded my life. Watching Edmund fight the drugs coursing through him makes me understand why such a power is addicting. Outside my door, I have dozens of people watching over me, but it was my willingness to take the risk which has put me in this position. Power is an illusion and using it against Edmund may give me a version of my life back.

"First, I want to thank you," I say and rise from my chair.

"For what? Making sure you're in pain for the rest of your life, you worthless..."

"Now, now. Disrespect is not a becoming trait," I say and step down from the dais, careful to stay out of his immediate reach. "And yes, for the pain. It has given me a focus. Reminded me I am alive. When I no longer deal with it coursing through my body, I will know joy like I've never experienced prior. It's a matter of perspective, I suppose."

"They were right. I should have killed you," he spits and lunges toward me.

I step back but do not escape the edge of his fingertips as they press against my ankle.

"Do you want me dead, Edmund? Like you wanted your contract owners dead?" I say as I make a wide circle around his body.

He shakes his head violently, but the action causes a problem, and he pushes his head into the carpet between his knees.

"Don't get sick on my carpet, boy. I'll make you lick it up," I snarl. "Now, tell me about how you want to do to me what you did to that Society couple."

Silence crawls across the room as Edmund struggles with the drugs coursing through his body.

"I did nothing to them," he says into the carpet.

"I'm up here."

He pushes up until he's on all fours.

"They told me I would pay if I didn't do what they wanted. The photos were Photoshopped, and they paid the couple off. I was forced to watch as they created the scene. Then the tribunal believed them. My entire life was ripped away," he confessed.

None of his words make sense. I sigh in frustration. "Okay. Let's say I believe you. Why stalk me?"

He sways but maintains his position. "I love you, but you abandoned me. Everyone does. I wanted you to see me," he says. "Then they told me I could have you if I could get rid of Reece. I wanted a chance."

I sigh in frustration. The man on the floor in front of me isn't the monster I ran from months ago. He isn't the demon in my nightmares. Nothing is adding up the way it is supposed to.

"It would never have worked between us," I say with defeat and step up on the dais. With care, I sit back down in my chair.

"I realize that now, Regent. You were born to rule," he says as his words lose form in a slur.

"You're mistaken. I wasn't born to do anything."

He shakes his head but closes his eyes. "Not everything is what it appears to be, Atlas," he says as he succumbs to the drugs.

Everything in me wants to scream. Instead, I raise my hand and the door bursts open as the room fills with a half-dozen people.

CHAPTER TWENTY-FIVE

"Atlas," Reece says with impatience. "Are you listening?"

"Yeah," I reply without thought.

"Lying isn't something I allow. Would you like to try your answer again?" he warns.

"Fine! No. I'm not listening. This whole damn thing is pointless. My hunch was pointless. This discussion is pointless!" I scream.

Reece stares at me with a raised eyebrow, but I don't even blink as I oscillate between anger and hopelessness.

"Your hunch and interaction with Edmund yielded more leads in an hour than we've done in months," Kade says.

"Who cares? I get it. He was a pawn, and we wiped him off the board, but I was expecting..."

"What were you expecting?" Reece asks.

"For this whole thing to be over. I want to wake up from this nightmare," I say as I push away from the table and rise to my feet. "All I want is my quiet life back."

Kade shakes his head.

"Your life was never quiet, Atlas. For as long as I've known you, the world around you has swirled with unsaid things. At first, I thought it was because your father was a ruthless businessman, but all of this makes more sense."

"I'm glad it's making sense to you, Thomas, because it makes little sense to me. If it's about power, they can have it. I'll give them the regency. My investiture hasn't happened, so some form of abdication is possible."

"You'll do no such thing," Dominick says as he enters the room.

I spin on my heel and face him.

"I'll do whatever I please. I checked my position and the authority which comes with it," I challenge. "Besides, based on rumors, you may not have my best interests at heart, anyway."

"True," Dominick agrees.

My mouth falls open in stunned silence at his admission.

"I have the interest of the greater good as my focus. You, like everyone else, have a part in keeping the whole thing running. I refuse to let a defiant, petulant girl bring down centuries of an underground civilization."

"Find someone else then." I step into his personal space.

"No. They chose you. I don't care if modern sensibilities let people shrug off their duties as easily as they shrug off a jacket. When you took on this mantle, you accepted its weight."

"Fuck you," I growl.

"At the pleasure of the Consort it would be my honor," he retorts without a blink. "Might I remind you, my dear Regent, your power is not absolute."

"Nor is yours, Counselor. You're not telling me everything here. Which means you are lying by omission," I counter.

"Welcome to the game, Regent. It's about time you showed up," Dominick says as he stares down at me.

I scowl and clench my jaw in frustrated confusion.

"I don't want to play this game of... whatever the hell it is."

"Then you should have thought about that before you put your piece on the board," Dominick says.

"It's hard to make good decisions when people omit pertinent information."

"Yes. I advised the same to someone a good bit of time ago, but it was decided that you needed to seek your own path. If things were put in front of you and you pursued them, then the path was decided. However, if you walked away, then you were released from the weight of it all."

I close my eyes and rub my temples. "For once in your blessed life, Dominick, can you just tell me what the hell you're talking about?"

"Do you remember when we met?" he asks as he takes a step back and walks over to a chair at the long table.

"Of course. You were my professor," I say with a shrug.

"More important, do you remember when we met for the first time in private?"

I scowl and shake my head.

"We'd just finished the unit on power and sexuality," he reminds me. "You were full of questions when you came by my office. At that moment, you had ample opportunity to walk away. I even advised you to do so, if memory serves."

The memory flashes across my mind.

"You made me wait nine weeks before you gave me the information," I whisper.

Dominick sighs. "Yes. No offense, but I was hoping I'd never see you again. Even when you agreed to be trained, I pushed you in the same hope, but you were stubborn. Worse, it is how you see the world. Even your father tried to distract you with vanilla business pursuits," Dominick points out.

"My father didn't know this world existed."

Dominick snorts. "It's time to take the blindfold off, girl. Who was your father's last companion?"

"Rob was his personal assistant and the closest thing he had to a companion. Mayra was his housekeeper and cook. They'd both been with him for over fifteen years," I reply.

"How did they react at his death?"

"They were... devastated. Almost more than me, but he left them both a generous inheritance," I reply, not following what any of this has to do with Dominick's insinuations.

"Contractees in a lifetime contract are often devastated when their contract owner passes, especially unexpectedly," Dominick says.

"You can't mean..." I start and then shake my head. "That's not possible. I would have known if it were... if they were..."

"How?"

"It would be different. The exchange or the interaction..."

"Would look like a formal relationship which had a base level of familiarity built up over the years they'd been together."

"He wasn't..."

Dominick nods. "He was the Regent's Consort. When your mother died in childbirth, he stepped to the very fringes of the Society, determined to give you the 'normal' life neither of them had as children. All the household staff were contractees."

"That's... it can't... I would have..." I say the words, refusing to complete the sentences running through my head. "I thought you said the position wasn't inherited."

"It's not. The Council chose you. If I were to guess, some thought you'd be easy to manipulate or that you would reject it outright because you didn't grow up in our world. Everything about you was equivalent to someone coming in from the soft world. There's no way to know why the consensus made this decision, nor does it matter. What matters is what you do now that you have a clearer picture of your world."

"You're an asshole," I reply.

"Indeed," Dominick says. "Now that your villain isn't so easily dispatched, how would you like to move forward, Regent? The world is full of darkness and terrors. It is how we move through such a world that matters."

CHAPTER TWENTY-SIX

"Okay. What is bombshells, Alex?" Kade quips. "Wait... that wasn't a Jeopardy question. Hmph. Anymore golden nuggets of 'Let's burn Atlas' world to the ground,' Dominick?"

"There's much Atlas needs to learn, and the first one is trust," Dominick says.

"It's hard to trust people who keep tilting your world," I reply.

"Such is life, Atlas. We are all built the way we're built. On behalf of many bad decisions we've made on your behalf, I apologize. However, you've made many of your own. The choice to walk away from the Society once you knew of its existence is on you. If you'd stayed, then much of this would have been easier. There is even the possibility you may have never been chosen to be Regent. It was your outside perspective, the knowledge of the soft world and vanilla inter-actions which placed you at the top of the list. Chalk it up to fate and move on," Dominick says.

"Kade, do you want to be my counselor? I think I'm done with this one," I say and level a glare at Dominick.

"With all due respect, Ma'am. There's no way in hell I'm taking on that position. Love him or hate him, and I can back your play on the hating him part right now, but he's the right person for the job. He will never take your crap, and he knows the politics. Based on our investigations, he's also one of the most versed in both the Society and the vanilla world, thanks to his professorship."

"I was afraid you would say that," I say with a sigh. "Okay. Do we have any answers from my time with Edmund?"

"Yes, Regent. In combination with our investigation, we know there's a power struggle within the Council. The good news is you already know the players. The bad news is I am beginning to believe the death of the last Regent was foul play," Garrett says without emotion. "In addition, after talking to Edmund a couple more times..."

"You mean interrogating?"

"I do," Garrett confirms. "We have some good news."

He looks up at Reece.

"They think there is a way to reverse at least some of your symptoms," Reece says.

I turn and look at him, refusing to let the hope in my chest bloom. "Explain."

"Edmund's sponsorship of the lab working on pain management was using the serum he injected into you as an inflammatory agent in the lab mice. They created it to mimic chronic pain reactions to help find a cure. Since it was synthetically created, they also worked on the antidote. That way, should one of them accidentally get injected, there was a way to stop the progression. The bad news is that it was based on immediate injection. No one knows if it will work once the serum has been in the system for a while. They recommend at least five rounds of antidote at two weeks apart."

"That's good news," I say with caution. "Why do I feel there is a 'but'?"

"Because nothing in your world comes easy," Reece says and offers me a smile. "But the antidote could cause excruciating pain, and there's nothing that will make it stop. In addition, you must be awake for the procedure to give the necessary feedback."

"I see a sadist created the cure."

"It may not be a cure. This is the part you must accept. You could go through the entire process and be worse off."

"Is there any other alternative?"

"Live with the pain, which may also increase over time. Continue to work with Dr. White to find some control."

"Well, this is turning out to be a spectacular day," I say with a laugh. "Anyone else have anything to add?"

"There is the discussion of your investiture," Dominick says from behind me.

"Anyone else?"

"You need to finish your household management plan and sign off on your security detail," Garrett says.

"Mr. Kinkaid, would you like to add to the pile?"

"Unfortunately, yes. We need to settle the business situations at the club and the PR firm. I'd also advise that you bring in your closest advisors and tell them exactly what is happening."

I nod.

"Last call. I mean, silence is compliance after all," I say to the room as I close my eyes.

"Atlas," Reece calls to me. "I have a very important question for you."

"Yes, Mr. Gabriel?" I say as I let out a deep sigh.

"Would you do me the honor of being my Regent and my wife?" he asks.

My eyes pop open, and I search for him until my eyes fall downward. There, kneeling before me, Reece looks up as he holds up a jewelry box. The square diamond is surrounded by sapphires. It is breathtaking as it catches the light.

For a long moment I stare at him. A thousand thoughts rush is as many directions.

"Why?" The question comes out in a rush.

Behind me, Kade lets out a chuckle.

"That's not the usual response to such a question, you know," Reece says as he stifles a grin.

"It's just... I mean to say..."

"Yes would be a great answer," Reece prompts.

I smile down at him. Everything I've ever wanted is wrapped up in this man. He's gone through hell and back with me. Yet here he is begging for more of it.

"Are you a masochist, Mr. Gabriel?"

"Based on my love for you, most likely, but I'd rather explore these positions in reverse," he says without moving. "Now answer the question."

"Yes," I whisper. "A thousand times yes."

"Good girl," he replies in the same tone as he works to rise from the floor. "Looks like you can add a ceremony to your ever growing to-do list."

"Well, that's one way to pile on. Are you sure you really want to be into this whole for better or worse thing? I mean, the worst can be pretty bad."

"I think I can handle it," he says and kisses me lightly on the forehead.

"Why do you want to do this? You've already accepted the position as my Consort." I look up at him with a little confusion.

"Your Consort rules over you, Regent. His responsibilities begin and end there. The job is to give you a respite, absolution and such, to lift some weight from your shoulders," Dominick replies for him. "As your husband, he gains more power. The Council can't overrule him in matters of your health, safety, or discipline. He loves you. These last few weeks have tortured him like no other."

"What he said," Reece says with a half grin.

I crease my brow in confusion.

"Let me make one thing clear. Ever since we were on the island together, I've wanted you to be my wife. You are an amazing woman. I am in awe of your grace and poise under pressure."

I guffaw. "You've not been paying attention recently, my Consort."

"We'll discuss such in private, but I assure you I've been paying constant attention. You don't need any one of the men in this room to help you succeed just because we are men. Each one of us is here because you want us here. You inspire our loyalty and commitment to you, but you don't demand it. How can I not want to return it when you hold my heart in your hands?"

With an effort, I blink at the tears, but they fall, anyway. I stare at Reece like he's the only one in the room. The surrounding silence is calm. There's a peace at the moment, and I never want it to end.

"I love you, Reece," I whisper. "Thank you for the honor of being your wife."

"No matter what is in front of us, we'll tackle it together."

I smile and let the world lift from my shoulders, if only for a moment.

CHAPTER TWENTY-SEVEN

"Ladies and gentlemen, please gather in the living room," James says in his familiar British accent.

I smile at both its familiarness and the unfamiliarity of it all. Across the room, the cityscape is muted in gray as a drizzle coats the city. It's been far too long since I've enjoyed this view of the city and a space of my own.

The small crowd gathers as my new world and old world intermingle while remaining separate. For as long as I can remember, this is exactly how my world was always perceived, but now it's time to change it if I am going to be successful.

"Thank you all for coming," I say to the group gathered in my apartment as Reece steps behind me and to my right. "The last few months have been difficult for every person in the room, either directly or indirectly. To that, there are no words to express my gratitude to each of you."

I force myself to breathe.

"You've got this, Atlas. I'm right here," Reece whispers.

"For far too long, I've carried secrets. Some were for self-preservation while others were used to segregate parts of my life. During our most recent crisis, I had to pull some of you in to my largest secret of all, which meant you kept it from those who were important to you. What I am about to say will be a shock to some and a shrug to others; regardless, I ask that you keep an open mind."

"Spill it already, Atlas," Samantha says from her seat on the couch.

"That would be Regent," Dominick says from behind her.

"Don't give her a big head, Dominick. She already thinks she's the queen of the world."

"No. That's Sophia Żak. Atlas is only in charge of the Americas," Dominick says with a smirk.

"Funny. Everybody's got jokes," Samantha replies with a shake of her head.

I take a long sip of my Scotch before continuing.

"Thank you for breaking the ice, Dominick," I say with a slight nod of my head.

"My pleasure, Regent. Glad to be of service," he replies, his tone sitting somewhere between playful and sardonic.

"As I was saying before I was interrupted, I am a member of an organization known as the Sovereign Society. We believe in the right of people to live in power exchange style relationships at all levels of their personal and professional lives through the use of legal contracts as a means of balancing the monetary game pieces within the larger civilized societies. These total power exchange relationships are balanced for the good of the contract owner and the contractee."

"Wait," Samantha interrupts, "you're serious?"

I nod in response.

"That's... slavery. Real life... slavery."

"Actually, it's more akin to indentured servitude, except it is consensual, negotiated and as balanced as humans can make it," I reply without emotion.

Samantha jumps up from her seat and stares at me. "How long? How long have you been a part of this... this... organization?"

I look up at Dominick. "The answer depends on your point of

view. Either all my life, which I was not aware until recently, or at the time I met Dominick."

She turns on her heel and glares at Dominick.

"This is your doing?" Samantha demands. "You sucked her into your organization and made the things in her books real, or is it that her books are real and being passed off as fiction?"

"Calm down, Samantha. There's nothing here to get worked up about," he replies and levels a hard gaze at her.

"Nothing to get worked up about? My best friend just told me she's part of some secret organization and has been since the beginning of our relationship. The entire time, neither one of you let me in on it? In what world did you think this was okay?"

"Samantha, please," I start.

"Don't. Don't say another word. At every turn, I was right there with you. Both of you. Yet, I wasn't... what?... Special enough to be let in on your little '*fraternity*'?"

"It's not like that," I say as I brace myself for the full force of her anger.

She looks over to Kade, who stands quietly at the other end of the couch.

"Did you know, Thomas?"

"I was recently informed," he says in quiet affirmation.

"I guess I'm the one left on the outside. I presume all the '*new*' people here are in on it?"

"Yes," I say with a nod. "Garrett is the head of my security, and Cassandra was working under both his and Dominick's guidance. Dr. White is working in an advisory position. The gathering at the club is the High Council, similar to part of a royal court."

"Unbelievable. I'm either stupid or you all are brilliant," she says as her glass slams down on the glass coffee table. "I guess the joke's on me."

"Samantha, please. I invited you here to be part of my life. Even if I couldn't tell you before, I'm breaking a couple dozen rules to tell you now."

"Part of your world? Why? Because you need a token peasant?"

"That's enough, Samantha," I say with a forcefulness I rarely invoke. "Be mad. Be pissed off. Feel whatever it is you need to feel for yourself, but do not dare put it on me. Keeping you in the dark would be far easier than letting you in. These people in this room are important to me, and last time I checked you are in this room. I am sorry you've felt slighted, or whatever negative connotation you are internalizing, but if I didn't want you here, I assure you, you'd never know this little get-together happened."

In front of me, Samantha stares at me. Her mouth hangs open in an expression between shock and awe.

"Who are you and what did you do with Atlas?" she asks, her voice a little meeker.

"I told Alexandra to kick her ass until she accepted help to lift the world. Then I demanded she assembles the best team she knew to do exactly that very thing," I say as I give her a smile.

"You've changed," she whispers.

"Indeed. Now the question to you is are you staying and walking through the looking glass with me, or would you like to be on the other side, in the world you know?"

"How does this change everything else?"

"I don't know," I say with a shrug. "It's why we are here."

Samantha looks pensive, and for a long moment I expect her to bolt for the door. For all of her outrageous activities, she needs an underlying stability, and I've rocked her world to its very core.

"Well, then I guess it will be a hell of a ride," she says, but her expression doesn't look convinced.

"Then please fasten your seat belt. Put your seat and tray table in its locked, upright position, and hang on."

Samantha shakes her head at me.

"I hope this ride has a good safety record," she says.

I shake my head. "Not recently."

A chuckle ripples around the room and dissipates the tension.

"Fine. I don't know how I can help, but it's better than being on the other side of the glass looking in, I suppose."

"Good call," Dominick says from behind her.

"Oh, you, Sir, are still on my shit list," she throws over her shoulder, and I laugh.

"Ian, do you have any immediate concerns, based on what I've said so far?"

He shakes his head. "I accidentally own a majority of a club, but as a friend, I'm here for whatever you need," he says, putting his hands up in quiet defense.

"I'll ask that you hang on to that majority and take good care of the club. I'm a little attached to it," I add.

"It will be my pleasure."

"Excellent. I love it when a plan comes together."

I look over at Reece and smile. He gives me a nod as I turn back to the group.

"Now, for some happier news. Mr. Gabriel has asked me to be his wife. Do you think we can pull it off in say... four weeks? That'll give me a chance to undergo a couple treatments for my... painful condition."

"Wait... back up... there's a cure?" Samantha asks.

"Maybe, but I'm not overly hopeful. There's a version of an antidote, but the process could be as terrible as everything else. It was meant to be given immediately; however, it's been weeks for me. There's no way to know if it will work."

"That's great! Right? At least it is some level of hope, especially with a wedding coming up. And four weeks? Are you crazy?"

"Not crazy, just pressed for time. Besides the wedding, there's an investiture ceremony to plan and a move to the Regent's compound. My to-do list was a little long the other day," I say and glare at Kade, Garrett, and Dominick. "But I think with everyone here, I'll get most of it done somehow."

"Hmm... you're moving? Any plans for this sweet apartment? I mean, Ms. McKenzie could use an upgrade."

"Cute," I say and shake my head at Samantha. "This location will be corporate housing, so to speak. A bit of a getaway for those who may feel stifled in their new roles."

"That sucks, but I suppose it's not a bad place to meet clients and such," Samantha says with a grin that tells me she's thinking of all the places she'll want to use with her various partners. "Looks like we've got a busy month ahead of us, but tonight-let's party!"

"That's the best idea anyone's had in some time, Samantha. There's much to celebrate," Reece says from behind me.

"James, play Samantha's playlist number ten," Samantha calls out to the room.

"You have ten playlists in my home automation system?" I say, looking at her incredulously.

"I've got thirty. Someone had to make sure James kept this place running... I think of it as payment," she says and flashes me a grin.

Music fills the apartment moments later.

"You're amazing, you know that?" Reece whispers against my ear.

"I don't know. Right now I am overwhelmed and scared of disappointing everyone in this room."

Reece sighs. "When this treatment works, the first thing I'm doing is taking you over my knee for a long overdue spanking. We'll consider a warm-up."

"Tease," I say as a shiver runs down my spine at the thought.

"Don't push me, girl," he growls.

"Yes, Sir," I say but refuse to contain the grin.

CHAPTER TWENTY-EIGHT

"Y ou look stunning," Samantha says from the door.

"Thanks. I'm so nervous."

"Why? The man at the other end of this walk is desperately in love with you, and he'll walk through hell for you. Few people get to know those things upfront."

I stare at the image in the mirror. The stark white sheath dress is accentuated with an embroidered belt in navy blue. In the center, the crest of my new position sits among other flourishes which repeat in long ribbon tails in the part of the dress that forms the train. It is the perfect nod to both my old and new life. While a delicate diamond band holds a long veil in place.

"How's your pain level today? Is there anything I can get for you?"

I shake my head. "It's down to an all-over ache, but not even it can ruin today." I smile at the mirror and watch her image walk toward me.

She places an arm around my waist and her chin on my shoulder. I sigh at her touch, glad for the progress of my condition.

"You've got this, and when you start bawling, I've hidden a linen handkerchief in your bouquet," she says, and her image grins back.

"How thoughtful," I say with a sideways grin.

Across the room, a male clears his throat.

"You two are breathtaking," Dominick says.

We both turn to face him, and I take in his tuxedo-clad, imposing figure.

"You clean up pretty good yourself, Professor," I quip.

"Thank you, my Regent," he says and offers me a slight bow.

"I will never get used to that," Samantha says with a shake of her head as she walks to the bed and picks up our bouquets.

"We'd better get going, or you will be late," he says as he glances at his watch.

"Brides can't be late," Samantha says. "Don't you know anything?"

"I know you need someone to rein in that sass of yours," he retorts.

"Many have tried. All have failed," she says as she heads to the door.

"Maybe you need a stronger stock," Dominick mumbles.

"That's enough sniping, you two. Today's about me. You know, the one in the white dress," I say as I step into the white satin stilettos.

"So needy," Samantha says with a laugh.

"Indeed," Dominick adds.

I shake my head with a deep sigh.

"Fine, let's do this thing," I say as I step toward the door.

Dominick doesn't move as I approach, and I look up at his face.

"I know a hand-fasting doesn't follow all the traditions, but since you're following most of them, I thought I'd complete the saying. Your dress is new, your headband is borrowed from the Society, and your sash is blue," he says as he opens a small jewelry box.

Inside are two small lapel pins, intertwined as they glint in the low light.

"These were the security pins your mother and father wore. I know you have little from your mother because of her position, but it is your position now. A local jeweler intertwined them to remind you of the bond between a Regent and her Consort. I hope you will let them be your something old," he says so low I barely hear him.

For a long moment I stare at the pins. Everything I knew about my parents has been turned upside down in the last few weeks, and in this box is proof.

"Thank you," I whisper and blink away the tears welling up in my eye.

Dominick passes me a handkerchief as I take the box from him.

"I'm not sure where..." I start.

"There's a small piece of fabric in the cleavage of your gown. I took the liberty to have it placed there so the pins, should you accept them, would be close to your heart," he says as he lifts the joined pins from the box.

I run a finger across the bustline of the gown and pull up the swatch of fabric.

"Here I thought it was a mistake," I say as I put the pins in place.

"Not everything is always as it appears, my Regent. Sometimes the smallest things can mean the most," he says, and I look up to see him smiling down at me. "Now we really should go."

"Thank you, Dominick. For everything. I don't know how I would have made it to this point without you."

"It is my pleasure to be of service, my Regent," he says with a slight bow and offers his arm as he steps through the doorway.

CHAPTER TWENTY-NINE

We walk through the club and toward the grand foyer in silence. Only the clicking of our heels punctuates the beat of our steps until we stand at the end of a small cluster of chairs. As the music changes to the beats of Vivaldi, every head turns toward us, and Samantha makes her way toward the front of the gathering.

My gaze meets Reece's, and the surrounding noise goes quiet. Beside me, Dominick takes a step forward, and I follow. Each step takes me closer to the one person who's been with me through every change until he learned exactly what I needed for the world to lift from my shoulders. In his arms I am safe, even when the world around me is in turmoil.

Dominick hands him my hand as Samantha takes my bouquet from me.

"Hello, beautiful," Reece says with a confident smile.

Everything in me shudders and relaxes.

"Hello, Sir," I reply in a hoarse whisper.

"Ready?"

I nod in response, afraid too many words will make me cry.

Reece turns to Dr. White and nods for him to begin. With one hand, he signals everyone to be seated.

"On behalf of Atlas and Reece, thank you for being here to witness the binding of these two lives within the recognized bounds of a power exchange. It is the duty of the Dominant to accept the submission of a willing partner. In return, the submissive accepts the guidance, discipline, and absolution of the Dominant. This exchange of power gives both partners what they need, want, and desire without the necessity to struggle. Do you have a symbol of your acceptance of this submission, Reece?"

"Yes," he says and pulls an affinity ring from his pocket as I offer my left hand to him.

"Atlas, it with great honor and privilege that I accept your submission. With all that I am I promise to love, honor, cherish and protect you. In every matter of our world, I promise to offer my guidance and grant you a place where my power will provide you a place of boundaries where my support will release you of your stress. With all that I am, these things I promise you. Take this ring as a symbol of this promise. Like a traditional ring, the completion of the loop shows my everlasting commitment while the symbolic locking screw holds it together just like our transfer of power binds us," he says and slips the ring on to my finger.

"Atlas, do you accept this declaration of power exchanged between you?"

I nod.

"Words, Atlas. I need your words," Reece prompts.

"I accept your symbol of our power exchange and the contract it represents... I... I... I am fully grateful for your dominance. I promise to always remember it is a gift and to treat it with the reverence and respect it deserves. Within our boundaries, I promise to love, cherish, honor, and obey you, knowing you care for my well-being and that your actions are provided to support me in all ways. May my submission always be shown in a way which makes you feel supported and trusted. By your chosen symbol, I accept our exchange of power."

"A Dominant needs not physical things to bind a submissive to him. When he takes time to offer focused attention to dominate her mind and give her a place where her world becomes his to lift, it is then that her body, and a willing heart follows. As witnessed before you today, in the culmination of these things she will willingly bind her soul to his," Jacob White recites. "It is with the greatest honor and privilege that we witness the binding of these two hearts, souls, and lives today. May I present to you Mr. and Mrs. Gabriel," he says to the crowd.

I drop to my knees before Reece as he bends down and kisses me on the forehead. In the next instance, he pulls me to my feet, grabs me around the waist, and kisses me like there is no tomorrow. Around us, the foyer explodes in a round of applause, but it is right here in his arms where my world falls blissfully silent.

CHAPTER THIRTY

R eece tucks an arm under my knees as he lifts me and carries
me through the door of my apartment.

"It's a good thing you kept your apartment, Mrs. Gabriel," he says
as he crosses the threshold.

"Is that so, Mr. Gabriel?" I ask.

He raises an eyebrow and looks down at me. "Indeed. We've got a
good list of unfinished business to which to attend now that your pain
threshold is at a much more manageable level."

"It's our wedding night, Reece. This can wait until another time."

He shakes his head. "No, it can't. There's no better way to start
out our commitment together than a round of absolution, girl," he says
as he sets me on my feet. "Besides, don't you want to see your gifts?"

"That depends," I quip.

His hand grabs a fistful of hair at the nape of my neck.

"What does it depend on, girl?" he whispers against my ear as a
shiver races down my spine.

"On your guidance and pleasure, Sir," I respond.

"Good answer. Now be thankful I don't make you crawl over

there," he says as he releases my hair and pushes me toward the living room.

"Ma'am, there's a priority one call for you," James says, his voice echoing through the room. I stop my forward motion and turn toward Reece.

"Silence notifications. Reroute calls," Reece says before I can answer. "I didn't tell you to stop moving."

I turn back toward the living room and continue toward the couch.

"Strip," he commands, only steps behind me.

Without turning around, I remove the short white dress I'd changed into before leaving the reception.

"Leave the garter and stockings on," he says when my fingers fall to the white ribbons.

I place the dress and bra on the coffee table and step out of my shoes. He'd already commanded that I wear no underwear on the way home. In the limo ride his fingers pushed me to the edge of an orgasm but refused to let it bloom.

Beside me, Reece sits on the couch and picks up the small wrapped box from the table. He hands it to me with a devious grin.

"Your wedding present, my love," he says.

My fingers tremble as I work the ribbon from the box. There's no hurry or hesitation to my movements as I lift the lid. Inside, a heart-shaped stainless steel blue jeweled butt plug gleams in the light, along with two Ben Wa balls and two pillows of lube.

"Over my knee. I want to see you wearing your present," he says and smiles up at me as he settles against the back of the couch.

I take a deep breath and pull my body across his lap as I place the box and its contents on the floor. His hand strokes my ass, and I moan.

"Is your body in a position to receive a spanking, Atlas?"

I nod, not trusting my voice.

"Words. I need words. They are important."

"Yes, Sir," I reply.

His fingers graze the pucker of my ass, and I shiver.

"Oh, we'll get to that shortly. For now, stare at them and count each stroke," he says as his hand lands across my ass.

I cry out in surprise and pain, but it blooms into warmth.

"Oh God..." I moan. "One, Sir."

Reece chuckles.

"I see someone needs this as badly as I do," he murmurs. "Welcome home."

"Thank you, Sir," I say and settle against his lap with a smile.

PLEA FROM THE AUTHOR

I am so glad you've reached the end of the book and hope you enjoyed it. Thank you for giving me your valuable entertainment time. It is readers like you who make writing such an amazing experience.

If you enjoyed the book, I hope you will leave a review.

Be the First to Know

Want news, pre-order announcements or stuff?

www.SapphariaMayer.com

Want to catch up on all my behind the scenes, current WIPs, side projects and early announcements? Become a Patreon of the Arts.

Sappharia Mayer's Patreons of the Arts

Feel free to reach out to me on any of my social media.

BB bookbub.com/authors/sappharia-mayer

twitter.com/sapphariamayer

pinterest.com/sapphariamayer

amazon.com/author/sapphariamayer

instagram.com/sapphariamayer

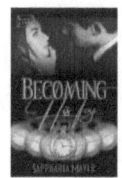

BECOMING HIS TOY
MIND GAME - HIS TOY COLLECTION (BOOK 1)

JOURNAL ENTRY

I can hear him in my mind now.

When I masturbate, I close my eyes, craving his voice, his command, his control. It soothes me and arouses me, making me dripping wet. The overwhelming desire for sex, just as intoxicating as anything I've put in my body to alter my reality.

It is the small voice in the back of my mind. Always present but not always driving. Waiting for me to accept the change and drop into his world. There- I am led. Encapsulated by his words. Pushed higher and higher in my mind while my body revels in its own desires. The edges blur and change of my identity. A relaxed state where everything merges and blends until it become the truth I am given.

His smooth velvet voice in a metronomic meter. It leads me down paths I would hesitate to go but secretly crave in the shadows of my mind. I give him everything he asks and want to offer more. The world *bursts into color now and each moment together creates a craving for the next.*

It wasn't always like this. There was a time when I survival and living were synonymous.

Until I met him.

And He set me free.

PRE-ORDER NOW! MIND GAMES : BECOMING HIS TOY

WHAT'S NEXT?

Atlas/Alexandra, Reece and Dominick will return in the Sovereign Society Series. There are so many more adventures when you realizes it's good to be the 'Queen' — *or is it?*

ALSO BY SAPPHARIA MAYER

ABOUT THE AUTHOR

Sappharia Mayer's erotic romance comes from years of experience in dynamic and various play in the BDSM/Kink lifestyle. She portrays the dance of power exchange relationships with a passion that pushes her characters, and readers, outside their comfort zone, making them squirm, cry, laugh and learn to see things in a whole new way.

Living around the metro area of the nation's capital gives her an up close view of politics and power on a global scale. She loves to delve deep into her worlds and indulge in her various passions, which may or may not include instigating fun *trouble* with her warped sense of humor. If you love romance with based in power exchanges with hot kinky sex, then check out Sappharia's books.

www.ingramcontent.com/pod-product-compliance
Lightning Source LLC
Chambersburg PA
CBHW020401210626
46816CB00006BB/2074